A
Harlequin
Romance

OTHER

Harlequin Romances

by VIOLET WINSPEAR

Many of these titles are available at your local bookseller, or through the Harlequin Reader Service.

For a free catalogue listing all available Harlequin Romances, send your name and address to:

HARLEQUIN READER SERVICE,
M.P.O. Box 707, Niagara Falls, N.Y. 14302
Canadian address: Stratford, Ontario, Canada.

or use order coupon at back of book.

THE PAGAN ISLAND

by

VIOLET WINSPEAR

HARLEQUIN BOOKS   TORONTO
WINNIPEG

Original hard cover edition published in 1972
by Mills & Boon Limited, 17-19 Foley Street,
London W1A 1DR, England

© Violet Winspear 1972

Harlequin edition published August, 1972

SBN 373-01616-6

Printed in Canada

1616

CHAPTER I

HEBE was restless, no longer able to sleep at night because dreams haunted her and woke her to tears on her cheeks and a sob in her throat. She began to prowl the seashore after dark, to try and find, perhaps, the ghost of Dion riding in on a wave at the helm of his yacht – eyes gaily laughing, green and carefree in a face almost unholy in its attraction. Her cousin, her close companion, her soulmate. The sun in her life, eclipsed by the breaking of a boom and a blow that knocked him into the churning sea and drowned him.

The gods take young the daring and the dancing!

And Hebe walked alone on the shore, while the wind sang like sad harps in the rigging of the yachts, where the *Halcyon* had once stood slim and racy.

Tears were unknown to the Lawnay cousins, reared together at the old Essex house called Memory. Whatever their hurts or their fears they had a gallant way of putting on a laughing face. But Hebe could no longer rely on her inborn gallantry to hold the newborn tears at bay. They came to her pillow and they drove her to secret places along the shore, where she angrily threw stones at the cruel sea and hated the thought of tomorrow . . . and yet again tomorrow.

Stars burned in the dark sky and the wind tangled her hair, silky like the hide of a cougar, golden and thick. Her lashes were darker, shading green eyes sad as tourmalines kept from the sun in dark velvet. Her mouth was lovely enough to be pagan, and her nose could take a scornful

5

tilt. She had beauty, but tonight, and ever since Dion's lean tanned body had been carried lifeless to the sands, her face was clouded and almost sullen, as if she blamed the gods and cried for them to take her to where they had taken her cousin.

She turned homewards, risking her ankles on the large rough stones of the shore. She tramped the path that led upwards to the old Norman church and there by the lych gate she stared at the pale, shockingly real figure of Christ on the cross. The old bells clanged, striking the hours. It was ten o'clock and she seemed to have the town to herself. Everyone else was snug indoors; the families and the friends were gathered around the small screen to watch a play or a film, and some were off to bed to read a book.

Hebe sighed and looked at the stars and wondered which belonged to Dion . . . then they swam together in a misty blur as the tears filled her eyes. "Don't cry," he would have mocked her, "or you'll scare the crows."

She went home to Memory and crept quietly upstairs to her room. Miss Prue, old nurse and faithful housekeeper, would be in her room at the other side of the landing, and Hebe didn't wish for cocoa and comfort. She wished to be alone with her sadness and her aching sense of loss.

If some other girl had taken him from her, then she would have jeered in the way of cousins, but she would not have been so bereft as this. Oh, to see no more that gay and rather wicked face . . . only in the snaps she had taken of him. To hear no more that gay and mocking voice, to run no more while he gave chase across the sand to the sea.

He had been fearless, and confident in his youth, and the gods punish those who dare to be like gods.

Hebe wandered restless around her room, picking up the small and valued things she had collected during the twenty years of her life and looking at them as if they belonged to a stranger. Some of them found with Dion in that quaint old shop that stood like a stopper at the foot of Sly Hill, where in the window stood small and fascinating oddments made of china and brass, porcelain and glass. It smelled of old things, that shop of cameo brooches, and jet necklaces. Of the aroma of coffee stealing down the stairs from the café next door ... Oscar's, where often after the play at the Castle they would go for supper to argue about the merit of the acting and the plot.

She picked up a tiny-faced lady in a strawberry-pink skirt and bonnet and she could hardly bear to remember that Dion had given it to her for her birthday. He had been twenty-one and a bit superior about it. A sigh broke from her ... and then she picked up the jewelled icon, and as her fingers touched its smooth frame, a strange message seemed to wing its way through her bones to her heart. Dion's father had wished him to return the icon to its rightful owner, but there had always been too much for Dion to do. He had never found the time ... but she had plenty of time ... days, weeks of it.

The great jet plane joined its shadow on the sunlit earth, and Hebe Lawnay was in Greece. She stayed the night in a hotel in Athens, and by mid-morning she was taking a look at some wonderful old ruins on a hilltop. After a hasty lunch she and her luggage were piled into a cab by a friendly doorman and the driver was told to take her to the quay where she was to catch the steamer to Petra.

Hebe sank back against the worn leather of her seat and

though she tried to relax her thoughts were too full of Petra, the island known in legend as the reluctant bride of the sun god Apollo, where the stone was golden as sunflowers. Her hand strayed over her handbag, which held in a flat leather case the icon that was taking her to the island called by the Greeks the garden of stone. She could visualise the flash of gems in the icon, the softly burning golden frame, worn smooth by the lips which had kissed it down the years. The last kiss it carried was her own, and it was strange, the compulsion to return it to Greece, as if Dion compelled her.

A little sigh came from her lips as she gazed unseeingly from the window of the cab. "Nikos must have the icon," he seemed to whisper. "You must find him and take it to him. His father fought in the war with ours, and though it was given as a gift, to bring luck, it must now be returned."

Yes, she thought, because the luck had failed . . . it had failed Dion, and she would give it back into the hand of Nikos Stephanos.

The family solicitor had made enquiries regarding the whereabouts of Nikos Stephanos and after several weeks it had been established that he was living at Petra after being resident for several years in the United States. Though it might have been easier for Hebe to send the icon to him, she had felt that this journey might help to lessen the pain of losing Dion. She was now alone, with only herself to consult, and the sale of the old house and its contents had made it possible for her to make the trip to Petra.

Miss Prue had gone rather sadly to live with her sister, and the house called Memory stood empty, waiting for its new occupants. Fiercely, in order to stem the silly tears,

8

she told herself it was a blessing to arrive when the weather was flawless, with a sky so blue it was dazzling. The smell of Greek earth, of tavernas and roasting coffee stole in through the windows of the cab as it twisted and turned among a maze of cobbled streets, making its way to the more isolated port from which she embarked for the island.

Petra, the stone garden, lay in the Ionian Sea, and she knew with her deepest instincts that the island would be unspoiled by tourism, by towering hotels and beaches packed with sunbathers. She wanted with all her heart to hear the shepherd pipes, the pealing of old sanctuary bells, and to smell the wild thyme and mint.

The Greek sun beat down on the roof of the cab and even with the windows open the interior felt rather like an oven. Hebe stripped off the jacket of her smart trouser suit, and felt the driver look at her from the corner of his eye. She had heard that Greek men were still a trifle old-fashioned when it came to women going about on their own, but Hebe was independent and desirous of her own company since the grievous loss of her cousin, her inseparable companion ever since childhood. No one on earth could ever replace him. Dion had been unique, and their affection for each other a curiously pure thing, bright as a flame.

Half an hour later the cab bumped over the cobbles of the waterfront and drove past some wooden sheds that smelled strongly of fish. It came to a halt and Hebe swung long legs to the ground and paid the fare. Her luggage was unloaded and she was so busy checking her various cases that it wasn't until the cab had driven away that she noticed the receding steamer, half a mile from the quay and on its way to Petra without her!

She stood at the waterside and gazed ruefully at the vessel as it grew smaller and smaller in the distance. She bit her lip and wished she hadn't given in to the impulse to see the ruined temple of Apollo before catching her cab. Well, standing here regretful wouldn't get her to the island, and she cast a hopeful look around her. A few tough-looking men were working nearby, but after a quick and curious survey of the foreign young woman in trousers, with her thick fair hair coiled at the nape of her neck, they continued with their task as if she didn't exist. Their skin was tanned and leathery from the sun and wind, but hers was a smooth white, and for once in her life she felt curiously helpless, rather like a moth which had flown off course into a semi-tropic garden.

With enquiring, green-tinged eyes she studied a tall Greek who stood alone on the quay, his entire attention upon the pipe he was lighting. He wore sea-faded canvas slacks and a shirt with the sleeves rolled above the elbows of strong-looking arms. Hesitant and yet in need of assistance, Hebe decided to approach him. Her Greek, thanks to her father, who had even named her after the cup-bearer to the Grecian gods, was quite adequate.

"*Kalispera*," she said. "Do you think you could help me?"

He glanced up slowly from his pipe and shook the flame from the match which had almost burned down to his fingertips. He looked at her with eyes so dark they were fathomless. He said not a word, he just looked, and she might have been one of the fish sheds for all the interest she evoked as a person.

"I have to get across to the island of Petra . . . is there another steamer making the crossing today? I should be very obliged if you could tell me."

He clenched his pipe in his teeth and his was a gaze filled with power, with elemental passions, and with suffering. It was a gaze hard to endure, and it took a lot of her courage not to retreat from him.

"The steamer has left for the day," he said. "There will not be another until the morning.'

"Oh . . ." She was disconcerted, by his dark gaze, by the information he had just imparted, and by the fact that he had an air of authority not in keeping with his rough clothes. "How unfortunate!"

"I am sure." Smoke curled from his lips and his gaze left her face and settled on the water. It was a look that almost dismissed her, and she felt temper coiling inside her. Was everyone in this outlandish place so impolite, so aloof, so careless of a stranger?

"Is there any chance of hiring a boat?" she asked. "I'd pay well."

"I am sure you would." His dark-browed, sea-deep eyes flicked over her, taking in the tailored suit she wore.

"Have you a boat?" she implored, and then despised herself for pleading with him. "If you have a boat and the time to spare . . . I'd be grateful for a lift to the island."

"You sound in very much of a hurry, but I hope you realise that Petra is extremely quiet and cut off from the usual amenities of tourist travel?" There was a cynical note in his voice. "Not many strangers visit the island. There are no hotels with hot running water and soft beds."

"I'm glad to hear it," she said, but his words and his manner gave her the feeling of having been stung and she was glancing around for someone else who might be more inclined to help her when he drawled:

11

"If you care to wait half an hour while I load the *Kara* with the provisions I came for, and they leave room enough, then I will take you." He shifted his pipe to the left corner of his mouth and once again his eyes appraised her, but there wasn't a scrap of flattery in them. "You don't appear to weigh much."

She flushed slightly. "I have several suitcases." She indicated them with a movement of her hand. "I have arranged to stay at the Firefly Taverna. No doubt you know it?"

"As I know most things on Petra. Be warned that the amenities are close to being primitive, and Lefkes and Maroula who run the place are rough and ready, and perhaps not accustomed to the ways of a smart young *Anglika*."

"I can assure you, *kyrios*, that I am not the demanding sort, and far from being put off by your description of the taverna I am relieved, and I look forward to making the acquaintance of down-to-earth Greeks."

"You will find my people unlike in many ways to your own people. Though Greece has been called the cradle of civilization, there remains in the blood of her islanders the primitive emotions and customs which might alarm a sheltered young woman from England."

"You must always have lived on your island," she said, "if you think English women so very sheltered. I assure you I'm not the nervous type."

"The independent type, eh?" A gleam of mocking amusement took fire in the depths of his eyes. "It must be galling to have to ask a favour of a man."

"I intend to pay you." She tilted her chin, which had a dent in the gently squared base of it. "And I hope you intend to let me?"

12

"You would dislike to be in my debt, eh?" He strolled away from her and her eyes widened with a delight that would not be denied as he began to load crates on to a blue-painted *caique* which was moored sternwise to the quay. Despite the master of the *caique* being a bit of a boor, she was glad she had lost the steamer. To arrive at Petra in a real Greek vessel was somehow fitting, and she would ignore the man and absorb all she could of her surroundings. The quayside itself was colourful, with the ruins of an old fortress half-way in the water, the half-submerged stones looking like lopped and savage heads. A black-hooded crow crouched on one of the stones, and a tangle of fishing nets held the glint of fish scales.

One would have to be a painter, Hebe thought, to capture the primitive appeal of all she looked at. The sun was reddening in the sky, and the wind sang low and harp-like in the rigging of the moored sea-craft. The unusual beauty of it all ran through her veins like wine . . . land of the gods, of sculptured ruins, pagan songs, and wine-gold seas.

"Come alive!" A pair of hard brown fingers snapped beneath her nose. "The *Kara* is ready to be underway, so let us see if you will fit in."

Hebe's eyes still held the hopes and reflections of girlhood when she glanced up at the master of the *caique*, and for a moment she looked rather lost. "Steady!" A hand gripped her arm and helped her aboard the two-masted craft, with a great eye painted on the side. "When did you last have a meal?"

"Y-you are becoming concerned about a girl." She gave a slightly nervous laugh and sat down on a crate, over which he had spread a gaudy rug. He brought her cases on board and stacked them around her, making a prisoner of her.

"If you were excited and in a hurry you might have forgotten to eat." The motor sprang to life and they moved away from the quayside, racing smoothly over the sea ripples which held like points of flame the rays of the westering sun. The profile of the Greek and his wide shoulders were outlined against the dramatic sky, and Hebe felt again the power and the mystery of the man.

"In my experience," he said, "most women are more concerned with their looks and their pleasures than the basic three S's."

"What are those, for heaven's sake?"

"Sustenance, sense and safety."

"You sound as if you consider women flighty."

"As birds."

His response was explicit, and after that for a while a silence fell between them and the *caique* rode gracefully the timeless seas of the Ionian. Though she had a motor she was sizeable, and her piratic, wind-tautened sails added a sense of romance to this journey. Hebe felt miles away from civilization, and for all she knew this stranger with his sunburned skin might be taking her anywhere. It seemed to her that there was something almost menacing in the pure, strong outline of his features, and clenched upon that pipe were teeth white and strong enough to eat a girl!

She smiled briefly at her thoughts, and breathed the wild and salty air of this sea of legend. Dion would have loved this boat and this moment, rapt and enchanted, held like a sacrifice between the flames of the sun and the deeps of the ocean. Then sadness clutched ... that half-hating of all life and all beauty since his life had been quenched.

How often had they talked of visiting the Grecian isles together, of coming to the country in which their fathers, who had been identical twins, had fought with the partisans. It was heart-rending that she came alone and the tears, like great jewels, burned in her eyes.

"I hope you don't mind the spray over the bows." The Greek spoke suddenly, and when she looked at him she was glad she had an excuse for the moisture on her cheeks.

"It's exhilarating," she said quietly, and she was wishing with all her heart that someone slenderer, with fair shining hair, stood in his place at the helm of the boat.

"You are a girl who seems unafraid of the sea." His words were as incisive as the cut of his features. "On that quay I somehow had a vision of having to hold your head over the side."

"Many thanks for your confidence," she rejoined. "As it happens I am used to the water and was taught to swim at an early age by my father, who was a naval commando in the war they call the second great one! You should take care not to jump to hasty conclusions about people, but I believe a great many men have a habit of doing so when it comes to women."

"You speak as if you are innocent about men."

She met his look and thought the skimming of his eyes "half darkness and half flame." There were sea-rough scrolls of black hair above those eyes, and he had a mouth that blended irony with iron will. He was in every respect an intimidating man, a real and hardy Greek, who must in his youth have been an Adonis.

"Not all girl make a hobby of having a lot of men friends. Some are content to –" She broke off; not to him could she talk about Dion and the devotion she had been

15

happy to give her cousin. Other young men had seemed tame in comparison to Dion.

Darkness was falling over the water now the sun had gone down, and looking at the Greek she realized how single-hearted had been her devotion, so that it seemed strange to be alone with him, and aware that she didn't know him to his very bones. She didn't know what would make him laugh, or what would anger him.

"You are on holiday, eh? You have come to bask on a Greek beach for a few weeks?"

"Yes, I intend to do some basking, and also plenty of exploring." She didn't mention the real object of her visit, for it had nothing to do with the master of a *caique*, who probably fished these waters and carried cargo. "Do you live on the island of Petra?"

"Yes, I reside there." He spoke distantly, as if he didn't wish to enter into details about himself.

"Have we much further to go?" Never before had Hebe been made to feel she was a burden, a bit of a child who talked a lot and bored her listener with her prattle. Colour rose and added its sting to her wind-whipped cheeks, and she hoped he would say they were almost at their destination.

"The run takes three hours and we are about halfway there."

"Oh dear . . ." Her heart sank, as well as her stomach. "I had no idea Petra was so far from the mainland."

"I detect a note in your voice, *kyria*, which tells me again that you have not had much to eat. Look, there is food below if you would like to go down the hatch to prepare it. We can eat it here on deck, if you wish?"

"I shall be even deeper in your debt, but I can't resist the thought of a meal." Hebe rose to her feet and moved her suitcases out of her way. Cutting the motor for a few moments, the Greek walked with a catlike precision to the bow of the *caique* and proceeded to light a pair of lanterns, one of which he fixed to a mast. He handed the other one to Hebe and pointed out the hatchway.

"You will find all that you need. Food, a frying pan, and a small stove which you light with a match, being sure not to have the burner too high."

"I shall try not to wreck your beautiful boat, *kyrios*." She had to smile, for he was so serious, and so determined not to unbend to the British stranger in tailored trousers and a jacket whose brass anchor buttons shone in the lantern light. Quite an omen that she should have bought such a nautical outfit for her trip to Petra!

She was wearing flat-heeled shoes, so she navigated the iron steps to the galley without a mishap. There she found everything in spanking order, as befitted a man whose face and head and every gesture spoke of pride, and perhaps love of his blue-painted *caique*. There were Greeks, she had been told by her father, who sometimes married from duty rather than love, and he might be one of those. Hebe knew he was married, for his left hand carried a plain gold ring!

As directed she lit the stove, filled the coffee-pot from a fat jar half-filled with ground coffee, and found a dozen eggs packed like figs in a biscuit-tin. A further examination of the larder revealed a tin of corned beef, and she decided to fry thick slices of it with the eggs. She would show her Greek Captain that she wasn't as totally inefficient as she must have looked, arriving at the quayside as the steamer departed, and having no other recourse but to throw herself upon the mercy of a stranger.

She found in a bread box a loaf the shape of a collar,

its crusty surface dotted with sesame seeds, and she sliced it into thick hunks. She was about to eat of the dark stranger's bread, and to quench her thirst with his coffee, but it was hardly likely to make them better friends. She was merely his passenger and when he landed her at Petra she would probably see no more of him.

Ah, canned peaches! They could have those to round off a meal that would be memorable for her, eaten on board an old and lovely *caique,* with its teakwood and its copper and its sails that took the sheen of silk in the setting sun.

After dishing up the eggs, discs of gold and white, miraculously unbroken, she cooked the beef quickly and covered the plates. Then she placed the coffee pot and mugs on the tray, emptied the peaches into a bowl, and prayed that in mounting the iron stairs to the deck she wouldn't trip and land at the Greek's feet in a nice mess of eggs, beef and peaches.

Luck was with her, and she felt the enigmatic sweep of the Greek eyes as he placed a crate between them for a table. "The food smells good," he said.

"I hope it will taste the same." She felt an odd rise of colour to her face, and it was a strange place in which to realise that the only other man she had ever cooked for had been her cousin. Never in her wildest dreams could she have imagined cooking supper for the master of a boat, in the midst of the Ionian Sea, and the strangest tremor ran through her as she set down the tray and uncovered the food. She spilled a little of the coffee as she poured it into the mugs. "I – I couldn't find any milk," she said. "Do you mind it black?"

"I prefer it black, if there is plenty of sugar. You take sugar, *kyria*?"

"Please." She sat down on one of the other crates, while

18

he lounged beside the silent motor to eat hungrily, with a fork, the three eggs, and the slices of meat, and to tear with his strong teeth the crusty bread. He must have been starving! And then, because she was hungry herself, she began to eat with a relish of her own this unusual meal.

"Good," he said, a note of amused surprise in his voice. "So you really do know how to handle a frying pan."

"Well, I'm no chef, but I can cope when it comes to a quick repast. You were ravenous yourself."

"Indeed!" He poured more coffee and stood gazing at the stars through the rigging of his boat, and Hebe was struck by something lonely about him. As he lifted his coffee mug the marriage ring gleamed on his hand, and she wondered what sort of wife let a man go hungry to sea. From the way he had eaten his supper it was obvious he had not eaten all day.

Hebe handed him the peaches, for she was replete herself, and content to listen to the water now the motor was still and the *caique* continued her journey under sail. The night was redolent of a pure freshness, so good after the heat of the day, and the strangeness of Athens. Here on the sea Hebe felt in touch with Dion, who had loved the water all his life.

Unaware, she sighed, and the master of the *caique* gave her a quick look, his dark eyes agleam in his still, strong face. "Greece sometimes calls the unhappy to her, like a goddess mother. Are you running away from a sadness? Or is it a too personal thing to ask?"

"No, Captain. Will your Grecian isle ease my hurt, do you think?"

"She will teach you, at least, that pain and sorrow are not confined to oneself. That each of us in turn must endure it. This is your first visit to Greece?"

"My very first, though my father and my uncle often talked of when they were fighters in Greece, helping the partisans. I have known all my life that one day I would come here. Is Petra beautiful?"

"For those who have eyes to see it, and feelings to sense it. Some say of the island that it is a garden of stone. That Apollo turned it to stone because Petra rejected him as a lover."

"Have you always lived there?"

"No – not always." That note of reserve returned to his voice, a firm warning that he had no intention of discussing his own troubles. "So your father and his brother were here during the war? They were brave, those who joined forces with the Greeks, and they are not forgotten by the islanders. What a pity your father is not with you."

"My father lives in Africa, where he works for the administration. When he and my mother went there I was thirteen and at boarding school, and somehow the years went by and I had no wish to leave England. I lived with my uncle and my cousin ... now I'm alone, and I expect at the end of my holiday I shall join my parents. We shall seem rather like strangers ... they love the tropics, and my mother teaches medicine."

Hebe paused and a fleeting smile touched her lips. "I'm not much like her ... I'm more of a dreamer."

"It is still good to have dreams even in this very realistic age. The dreams and the legends still linger in the isles of Greece, and it is well known that no matter how far a Greek travels like Jason in search of the golden fleece, he will if he can return to his native land to enjoy the last of his years." With these words the motor came to life again, and the *caique* was driven faster over the waves, as if her master regretted the time he had lost in eating with

20

his female passenger, and talking to her of Petra, and the parents she had not seen for such a long time.

She was about to stack the tray and to take it below when he said, crisply: "Leave them for now. Take a rest, for we have quite a long way to go, and it is good to count the stars while you have the chance. The sea and the stars are twin souls. One is so deep and the other so untouchable."

Hebe spread the Grecian rug and curled up like a slim, obedient cat. Dion had often told her that she had many of the ways of a cat, though her claws were always sheathed. With him, yes, but once or twice in the mysterious company of this Greek she had felt them stretching and curling, as if there was in his nature something not in tune with her own. A certain arrogance, perhaps. A brusque refusal to unbend to a woman . . . as if to a Greek a woman was a lesser being.

CHAPTER II

HEBE had fallen asleep, only to wake suddenly as hands firmly gripped her shoulders, and her eyes opened to find the face of a man bent close to her. "Dion!" her heart cried, and his name was on her lips a moment before she realized that the mast light played over hair like night, depthless dark eyes, and an unsmiling mouth.

"We have arrived," he said. "We are at Petra."

She sat up hastily and as she did so the strong hands slid down her arms and seemed to leave a trail of fire. He towered over her, and still rather confused, Hebe stood up, and then almost fell because her left leg had gone numb. "Oh . . ." Again he gripped hold of her and she felt a fool. "I – I lost my bearings for a moment . . . thank you." She stamped her foot and the life tingled back into the limb.

"You are sure? I don't want you to fall down the gangway."

"I'm fine." She pulled quickly away from him, and had the panicky feeling that if he had held on to her she would have fought furiously for her release. She didn't like her ingratitude, but now they had reached the island she wished to get away from him as soon as possible. He made her feel uneasy . . . his hard capability seemed to bruise her, wrenched as she was from the security of having Dion for her shadow and her sunlight. It was almost an affront that another man should be so alive, so vital and invulnerable.

She turned and found her jacket and put it on. She picked up her handbag and snapped it open. "I had better pay you now," she said. "We might not see each other after tonight."

There was a decisive click and her bag was shut again, and his fingers lay firm over the clasp. "A Greek does not take payment for a favour. I was returning to Petra, so it cost me nothing to bring you."

"You gave me supper."

"You surely paid for it by cooking it." His smile was a brief twist of the lips. "It is time to go ashore. If you will take the smaller case I shall bring the others."

She obeyed him in silence and wished that she had the courage to leave money behind to pay for the trip. She didn't wish to be in his debt, but she knew enough about the Greeks to know that only by the return of a favour would the slate be cleared.

"Come!" He spoke as if to a slightly obstinate mule, and pressing her lips together Hebe followed him down the planking to the shore. The *caique* was moored in an inlet formed by a halfmoon break in the rocks, and she smelled the drifting fragrance of pine trees as she stepped on to the sands of Petra. Hebe had not expected her arrival to be in the company of a man whom she hoped was not a typical islander. She wanted to find a welcome here, and hoped that the household of Nikos Stephanos would be a friendly one.

"Is it far to the taverna?" she asked.

They walked across the beach, heading for the low glimmer of lights outlining the harbour, a mere cluster of boat sheds and tiny houses of stone. Beyond lay hilly streets, the ghost-white walls of a church, and a large lan-

23

tern winking green and red, catching the eye and beckoning the traveller as it hung in the night above the harbour.

"There," said the Greek, "the Firefly Taverna."

So near, and yet possibly two hundred steps away, and Hebe wanted to arrive there as soon as possible, so that she might thank the master of the *caique* for his hospitality, and turn away in relief from his hard, detached figure. His very aloofness was ice against her spine. He made her feel his stony indifference with every glance he gave her.

Up and up the worn and winding steps they mounted, until the firefly lantern grew less mysterious and the shape of the inn came in sight. They arrived at last and Hebe sagged against a wooden porch and gave a breathless gasp. "What a climb! No wonder you Greeks are lean as wolves!"

"Had you caught the steamer there would have been a donkey for you to ride uphill. You should learn to be punctual, *kyria*."

"Blame my late arrival on Apollo," she rejoined, and without explaining further she swept in through the doors of the taverna and was met by a smell of sage, onions and coffee, and the stare of a woman darning a sock.

"Maroula, *gia sou*. I bring you the young *Anglika* who should have arrived much earlier on the steamer. She tells me she has a room booked here." Hebe's suitcases were set down by the tall Greek in his coat of shaggy sheepskin, and a look of amazement was on the face of the woman named Maroula, who dropped the sock to the table and rose from her chair.

"*Ne,* we were expecting another guest. It was good of you, *kyrios*, to bring the young lady. You will take a glass of *ouzo*?"

24

"*Evkaristo,* but not right now. I have to be on my way home or my Ariadne will be anxious." He glanced at Hebe. "I hope you enjoy your visit, *kyria,* and that our island consoles you. Maroula will take good care of you, and now I bid you goodbye."

"*Adio, kyrios,* and my thanks for bringing me to Petra. I am grateful, and I hope I was not too much of a bother?" A faint smile glimmered in her eyes, and she had to tilt her head in order to look at him and this made her face, with its hint of sadness, seem like a votive offering to some pagan deity . . . the Greek was so dark in contrast to her fairness, so self-contained and aloof. Any other two people who had shared supper together beneath the stars might be friends by now, but there was not a sign of it between Hebe and this man. He was as withdrawn as on the quayside when she had first spoken to him.

"*Adio.*" With an abrupt nod at Maroula he withdrew from the taverna and the doors swung shut behind him. For a moment there was a sort of lull in the atmosphere, a strange pent peace, with a kind of dullness to it.

Then Hebe looked at her hostess and felt not unlike a child delivered for the holidays and left to do what she could about enjoying herself.

"You must wish to see your room," said Maroula, "but first will you sign the book and I will call Lefkes to carry your luggage upstairs."

Hebe followed Maroula to the desk, where in an old leather book she signed her name beneath that of a Mrs. Daphne Hilton, no doubt the visitor with whom she would have travelled on the steamer had she been in time to catch it.

"I see there is another English woman staying here," she smiled at Maroula.

"The other lady is an American, from the city of Boston, she told us. Extremely chic, and rich, I think." The dark eyes flickered over the trouser suit which was now much crumpled after being slept in on board the *caique,* overcrowded as it had been with crates of goods. A tingle of embarrassment ran through Hebe. It would not be considered proper by a Greek woman to arrive this late at Petra in the company of a *caique*'s captain, and yet there were aspects to that rather strange journey which Hebe would have been sorry to miss. It somehow seemed appropriate that a man of stone should bring her to the garden of stone.

"You would like something to eat before you go to bed?"

"I had supper on the boat, thank you. All I really want is a bath and my bed . . . would it be possible to have a bath at this late hour? It was so hot in Athens and I feel tacky after that long journey across the water."

Hebe smiled so coaxingly that some of the starch went out of Maroula, whose sun-lined face broke into a reciprocal smile. "The American lady had a bath, and there should still be some hot water in the tank. Come, I will show you the way."

They went up a flight of twisting wooden stairs to the second floor and Hebe was first shown her bedroom, and then the rather quaint old bathroom, with a tub which was almost Victorian, and a brass tank on the wall which presumably housed the hot water. "'The *kyria* has only to turn the taps and water will pump into the bath." Maroula smiled with obvious pride in the amenity. "I will fetch clean bath towels and ensure that all is well with your room."

Hebe soaked for half an hour in a lukewarm bath and

gazed with half-closed eyes at her toes as the water slowly drained away. She felt in a curiously divided mood, as if one half of her was still in her native land. Everything smelled strange, and hardly anything bore a resemblance to the things she had known and lived with for twenty years. Faces had a pagan distinction that imprinted themselves upon the mind like sculpture, the Greek voices had a dramatic quality, so that omens and poetry seemed to be hidden in every word. She was glad that she had come, yet sorrowful that she had had to come alone.

Tired out by the events of her first long day in Greece, Hebe slept like a child, and those haunting dreams were held at bay for the first time in weeks. She awoke utterly refreshed to find sunlight striping the whitewashed walls of her room, coming in through the gaps in the weathered shutters. She sat up stretching her arms, and it was almost with guilt that she felt a sense of aliveness and anticipation. Her eyes grew sombre again and she wrapped her arms about her knees and stared at the tigerish stripes made by the Greek sunlight. She had known, of course, that her youth would reassert itself and her tendency to brood over Dion would lessen, but it seemed like a treachery.

She gave a start as knuckles suddenly rapped her door. It opened and a girl appeared, carrying a tray, and wearing a tentative smile. When she saw Hebe, young and slim in the bed, her fair hair ruffled above a pair of enquiring green eyes, the girl broke into a wider smile.

"I am Katina," she announced. "I work here, and I bring your breakfast."

"How do you do, Katina." Hebe smiled in return and accepted the tray across her knees. "*Evkaristo*."

The girl opened the shutters and the sunshine literally

flooded into the room. "The day will be a good one, a golden day of summer. Does the *despoinis* plan to go swimming?"

The English Miss drank her dark and delicious Turkish coffee and examined the contents of her breakfast tray. Three fat grilled sardines with toast, and a cheesecake, hot and herby, with slices of watermelon. Youth and appetite ran like quicksilver through her veins, and she shot a considering look at Katina as she buttered toast with a lavish hand. She had to ask someone about Nikos Stephanos and a girl in her own age group might be more forthcoming than Maroula.

"As a matter of fact I have come to Petra to see someone. The son of a man who knew my father. I think today that I shall try and see him ... he is named Nikos Stephanos."

Katina raised dark eyebrows, and the sun struck across her hair, turning it to the sheen of wild plums. "The Kyrios Stephanos is the rich man of the island. He lives in the biggest house, and with his partner he builds boats. He is not of much company ... he keeps apart from people and his house is a secluded one, with a keeper at the gate."

Hebe ate smoky sardine and buttery toast, and felt a trifle chilled by this portrait of the man she had come so many miles to see. "Does he live alone?" she asked. "Somehow I pictured him with a family, but he sounds instead a recluse on a hilltop."

"The Kyrios Stephanos had a wife, but they say he killed her ..."

"What?" Hebe gazed at Katina with startled eyes. "Is the man a murderer?"

Katina raised her hands and let them drop again, in a significant gesture. "He said she fell from the Rock of

Helios, but some have whispered that he pushed her. Everyone knew that she did not wish to live in Greece . . . the wife of his partner gave evidence about it . . . but his wife was so slim and golden, like a child, and he is big and dark, a man of temper, and it is in the Greek temperament to accept that a man may have his reasons for raising his hand against his wife."

"You mean," Hebe whispered, "that it was never proved that he didn't raise his hand and cause her to fall?"

"They were alone when it happened. He is a member of a powerful and influential family, therefore he walked from the inquest with an unbowed head. He should never, people said, have married a foreign girl. A Greek should marry with a woman of Greece."

"Was she English?" Hebe asked, intrigued by the story despite her feeling that it was going to be dangerous instead of nostalgic to meet the son of her father's friend.

"No, she was an American. They lived there and had a child there, and then all of a sudden they returned to Greece and Kyrios Stephanos bought the big white house among the lemon groves, which had already a sad history, and a man in leather boots guarded the gate, and the Kyria Stephanos was never seen out alone. The child was left in America with her grandmother, but after the tragic death of the *kyria,* the *kyrios* went to fetch her from America. Now they live alone at the house except for servants, and sometimes a governess comes, and then goes away again. Some feel sorry for the *kyrios,* but I shiver when I see him. He is taller than a real Greek should be. His eyes are so deep and dark they cannot be read. He never smiles."

"You sound, Katina, as if you don't much like Nikos Stephanos, yet his father was a hero of the partisans." Hebe had to attempt to be reasonable about this man she was destined to meet. "Gossip can sometimes make black what is merely grey. He and his wife might not have been happy together, but –"

"But it was a *love* match," Katina broke in. "Everyone knew at the beginning ... he fell madly in love with this American girl, to the big disappointment of his family, who had hoped that he would marry his cousin, a real Greek girl named Kara. It must have been something very bad, perhaps another man, which made him angry enough to –"

"There was no evidence that he caused his wife's death. If there was another man and Nikos Stephanos wouldn't let her go, then perhaps she did jump to her death."

Katina considered this, but being young and pretty she obviously could not visualise doing such a thing. "He looks, *kyria*, as if he could kill!"

"Looks and actions are not quite the same thing." Yet even as Hebe spoke she was wondering if, after all, she wanted to call on Nikos Stephanos with the icon. It didn't sound as if he'd be all that happy to see her ... anyway, she'd have a wander around the island this morning and maybe try and get a look at his house before attempting to go near it.

"Well, that was a very nice breakfast, Katina, and now I'll go and wash, and when I've dressed I'll take a look at Petra."

"What will you wear, *kyria*?" Katina opened the big, old-fashioned wardrobe and examined its contents. Hebe had brought summer frocks and slacks, and a couple of evening dresses, but they hung in a rather pathetic bunch in that enormous piece of furniture. "The American lady has a great many clothes ... Maroula says she must be quite rich."

30

"Well, Katina, I am reasonably poor." Hebe spoke with a slight laugh as she slipped into her robe and took her toilet bag from the dressing-table. "Would it be possible for my trouser suit to be pressed? I shan't be wearing it today, but I travelled here on a *caique* that was rather laden and I got a bit crumpled. I missed the steamer, you see, and I was lucky to find a captain who would give me passage to Petra."

"This is the suit?" Katina held the willow-green trousers against her and gave a giggle. "If I should wear such a garment my father and my brothers would burn it! Greek men are so strict in some matters, but I have heard that the *Anglika* is free to do as she pleases. Is this true?"

"Just about. We are not restricted, but I sometimes wonder if we are entirely happy. Are you happy, Katina?"

"I think so." Katina gazed with dark and wondering eyes at the English girl. "Are you not so, *kyria*? Are you all alone? Have you no brothers or sisters?"

"I had a cousin . . ." Pain twisted across Hebe's face. "Will you press the suit for me? I will pay you –"

"I will be pleased to do it for friendship." A carnation pink ran beneath the olive of Katina's clear skin. "I like you, *kyria*. You are much nicer than the American lady. She does not ask, she demands."

It seemed an apt description of so many women of the world, and Hebe was pleased and touched that she should be thought different.

After returning from the bathroom, which had been strongly redolent of expensive body lotions, no doubt used by the other female visitor to the taverna, Hebe examined her wardrobe and decided to wear a tangerine-coloured dress, sleeveless and utterly plain, and a pair of comfortable beige sandals that would be easy on her feet. She combed her hair as smooth as a cap and clipped it at the nape of her neck with a bronze buckle. She ran a light coating of sun-cream over her face, and applied pale tangerine colour to her lips. She studied her reflection with candid eyes, and then on impulse she transferred the icon from her leather bag to a raffia shoulder-bag. And she also tucked into it a nylon scarf.

The household of Nikos Stephanos sounded a tragic one, and Hebe found herself feeling sorry for the child who had been dragged from the bosom of her American grandmother to a house of shadows in a grove of lemons . . . a golden fruit that grew on dark trees!

Hebe swung about and walked from her room. She closed the door and ran down the stairs to the lounge of the taverna. A lean Greek with a full moustache was polishing glasses behind the bar. "*Kalimera*," he greeted her, and though he didn't stare at her, she felt as if not a detail of her dress and person had been missed. "I am Lefkes, and I hope, Mees Lawnay, that we are making you comfortable?"

"Indeed you are. I slept soundly and enjoyed my breakfast very much. I am now going for a stroll in all that wonderful sunshine. What time should I return for lunch?"

"Between one and three o'clock. We serve coffee at eleven if the *kyria* should wish to return at that time."

"It will depend." She walked to the doors, which were wide open to let in the air and the sunlight. The inn was old and weathered, but it was spotless. From her father and her uncle Hebe had heard that the Greek people were the essence of cleanliness even though they were often very poor. She smiled at Lefkes. "Though the sun is so brilliant the air is fresh. It's a wonderful combination."

"It is the *meltemi,* which blows from the mountains and keeps the air of Petra like wine." Lefkes fondled his bandit's moustache and smile-lines ran in all directions over his swarthy face. "Beware of Petra. You will lose your heart to her, as Apollo did."

"I am sure I shall." Hebe stood on the threshold, caught between the sunlight of the street and the shadow of the taverna. "Lefkes, is it far to the house of Nikos Stephanos?"

At once the smile was gone from his face and his moustache seemed to bristle. "The *kyria* cannot mean to go there? Visitors are not made welcome at the Villa Helios."

"Helios!" she gasped. *From the Rock of Helios the wife had fallen.*

"House of the Sun Lord."

"And you don't advise me to go there?"

"The house, so people say, should be dedicated to Hades."

"The dark lord of torment." Hebe could feel the quickening of her pulses, the wish to dare and defy the superstitions of the islanders. If the man had really killed his wife he would not have walked from the court of inquest a free citizen. The law was not that easy to break in any land, even one which raised the man higher than the woman.

"Is the man such a monster?" she murmured.

"He walks about the island like other men, he takes his wine and does his work, but people whisper when he passes. Maroula was quite –" There he broke off in midspeech as a member of the staff entered the lounge. Hebe escaped into the sunlight and hurried away before Lefkes could detain her with further anecdotes about the notorious Nikos Stephanos.

33

From all accounts his house was above the streets, among the hills of the island, with white walls among the dark green foliage of the lemon trees. She had to take a look, even if she didn't have the nerve after all she had heard to approach him with the icon. She could feel the weight of it in her raffia bag, an object of pagan worship set with gems, which had become associated in her mind with misfortune. Perhaps those pagan gods wished it back in the household of this man whose wife had died so strangely. Many things seemed possible in this land where the gods had walked.

On her way to the hills Hebe passed cavernous doorways set within walls of rough stone coated with whitewash, so that the effect was one of black and white, like the ancient patterns on Greek vases. She saw great fat waterjars beside the doors, and windowsills thick with pots of herbs and plants. A man passed her going down the street steps, rings of sesame bread straight from the oven threaded on his arm. There were melon beds wherever the sun fell, filling the fruit with a Greek ripeness, and sometimes the weird sight of octopus drying in the sun. A donkey munched carrots beneath an archway, blue beads and tiny bells jingling around its neck.

Beads and bells to keep away the evil eye, and one old woman all in black, from her head shawl to her stockings, who crossed herself as the English girl passed by with her bare arms and the sunlight in her green eyes.

Dion had once remarked that the true sign of a witch was the green of her eyes, and then he had quickly kissed the nape of her neck. Hebe gave a tiny shiver, recalling the feel of his lips, a flame quenched by the sea.

Soon she had left the streets behind her and was following a hilly path marked by the cloven hoofmarks of

34

ewes, brought to the plateau to feed on the grass clumped in the shade of the boulders. Petra, the stone garden, with a sheen to it of honey and pale wine. A scent of blue sage and thyme mingled in the sunlit air of the *meltemi*, and the drunken purring of a million cicadas intensified the solitude, Hebe's alone, for the ewes were far down the other side of the hill, a distant chime of neck bells and the occasional plaintive bleat.

Hebe took a deep breath and the air of Petra seemed to flow into her veins like a wild wine. The uneven rhythm of the cicadas was like the excited beat of her heart, and the soft wind caught at her hair and carried a strand of it across her lips.

She scrambled further up the plateau, and she didn't know whether she was fleeing from the unseen presence of Helios, lord of the sun, or hurrying to him. She heard a new sound, like a thousand teardrops falling upon stone, and the breath caught in her throat as she reached the summit of the hill and saw a waterfall breaking in silver spate against the rock as it tumbled and fell from the side of a shelf of golden stone, clustered round with locust trees and judas, twisted olives and wild lemon.

As if seduced, and unable to help herself, Hebe stepped upon that golden shelf and stood there like a tawny young goddess, or a green-eyed witch, and watched entranced as the water fell downwards, tumbling in all its silvery freedom over the rocks, down into a gorge as deep and dark and bottomless as sin itself.

Ferns were thick about her ankles, and the cry of a bird as it flew across the sky was like her heart crying, both sadness and joy. She sank down on the stone, among the ferns, the red splash of poppies, and the anemones of Adonis. She felt almost like a sacrifice to all this wild

35

beauty, and she felt a reluctance to continue her search for the shadowed house of Nikos Stephanos. She wanted to stay here and dream of Dion, who would have gloried in that waterfall, the tears of the many maidens sacrificed to love.

On an impulse she opened her bag and took from it the icon in its leather case. She opened the case, and the two golden leaves of the icon and the topaz gems caught the sunlight and flashed like a tawny fire. Within the frame of gems was a haloed saint ... St. Nikos, for whom the unsaintly son of a war hero was named. It seemed a blasphemy, if all that was said about him was true ...

Suddenly her whole body seemed to go taut and her hand clenched the icon as she glanced wildly about her. The ledge of rock on which she sat, overlooking a gorge into which fell the quick, cool water, had something significant about it, almost the look of a pagan altar ... to Helios, lord of the sun!

The realization struck her like a blow ... the rock upon which she reclined was the same rock from which the wife of Nikos Stephanos had been pushed, or from which she had fallen. Hebe's sense of peace was abruptly shattered, the beauty was blighted, and with a strangled cry she leapt to her feet and in so doing the icon fell from her hand and dropped down the sheer side of the rock, flashing through the sun into the darkness of the gorge.

"Heaven help me!" Hebe gasped aloud. She knelt and peered downwards and saw the distant glimmering of the icon, caught by its golden leaves on the branch of a shrub. A goat-footed shepherd lad might manage the climb, but Hebe didn't reckon she stood much chance of retrieving the icon without breaking her neck.

"Can it be possible," spoke a deep voice above her head,

"that the *Anglika* is in need of assistance so soon again?"

She twisted around, startled, and looked not unlike the naiad of the falls as she lay there gazing up at the dark figure who stood so tall against the skylight. His features were firmly sculptured, as if bronzed. His eyes were as fathomless as she remembered them, and close as fleece was his black hair. An indigo shirt was open at his brown throat, and the lean length of him was intensified by the narrow black trousers he wore. His feet in thong sandals were firmly planted in the ferns at either side of her.

He stood above her like doom itself . . . and suddenly her heart was in her throat.

"Captain!" The word broke from her. "You walk like a cat-burglar!"

"I may be many things," he rejoined, "but I am not yet a petty thief. You appear to have lost something down the gorge."

"A valuable icon . . . it doesn't really belong to me, so I must try and retrieve it, somehow."

"You seem doomed, *kyria*, to lose things." He regarded her with a frown, then abruptly he lowered a hand for her to grasp. "Come, you are very near the edge and you don't want to follow the icon."

She stared at his hand, sunburned, strong with the tough texture of a seaman's skin. It wasn't from the honest toil that she shrank, it was from the man himself, appearing as if from out of nowhere to find her once again in a predicament.

"I – I can't leave the icon down in the gorge, Captain. I came all the way to Petra to give it to a certain person . . . it's many years old and . . ."

"You will not be many years old if you fall to those rocks." And her cry was lost in the sound of the cascade as the Greek swept an arm about her and lifted her bodily from the ledge. For brief moments as he swung her to safety she was unbearably close to him, locked between the vigour of his forearms, with dark hair fleecing the firm muscles. She felt potently the mysterious power of his personality, the absolute pride of the true Greek, and she saw also the pull of a muscle in his jaw, alive and tense beneath the skin that was bronzed by the sea winds.

"I believe this place has a bad reputation," she said, and the words came huskily from a dry throat.

"Evil," he said succinctly, and he forced her to move further still from the ledge, so that glancing back at the Rock of Helios it did seem a perilous place, a rough golden throne, with the poppies splashing it like drops of blood.

"But what of the icon?" She looked at him and the dark eyes seemed to smoulder dangerously in the lean face clawed by sun lines. She knew he was thinking of the tragedy which had occurred here, and why this part of the island was so deserted. Greeks were of a superstitious nature . . . but what, she wondered, had brought him to the spot this morning? Had he from a distance noticed her dress? Had some instinct told him that only the foolish stranger whom he had brought to Petra on his *caique* would come to this place, which for the islanders was haunted?

"No one will fetch the icon up from there, will they, Captain?"

He made no reply but continued to clasp her waist with his hands, almost as if he had forgotten he held her so, and his features were so still, like those on a Grecian frieze, with a purity and a menace to them. Hebe stood as still as he and the thought struck her that he was a man to whom happiness was just a word. She glimpsed in his eyes aeons of joyless days, and nights, felt it in his touch and in her own inclination to pull away from him.

Close to him like this her every nerve cried *danger*. Perhaps because he was older than Dion had been, no longer a boy but a man whose spirit seemed scarred by some bitter experience beyond even the suffering she had known when told there had been an accident and she had run all the way to the beach, only to find the light and the laughter gone out behind the closed eyelids of Dion.

"Come," he spoke abruptly, this man who was so strange and different from Dion. "I am sure you would like to get away from this place."

"But the icon!"

"It will be retrieved, I promise you."

"Who will dare to go down there?"

"There is always someone, but it could not be done without a rope."

"I shall pay, of course. The climb looks a dangerous one."

"You are always insistent about settling your bills," he drawled. "Does it actually give you a pain to accept help from a man . . . what are you afraid of, that he may demand payment from your lips instead of your cheque book?"

"He would be unlucky!" She retorted with spirit, but her skin felt as if it lost colour . . . it couldn't help but cross her mind that a girl could be easily overcome by a man in so lonely a place, with no one about but the ewes to hear a cry.

As if reading her mind his mocking eyes scanned her face until they settled on the sensitive curves of her mouth. "Would you like to repay me now for bringing you to the island?" he asked laconically.

"With a kiss?" she gasped.

"Why not?" His head came lower, to meet hers, and the breath caught sharply in her throat as she looked into eyes that seemed to smoulder with deep, adult fires.

"Don't . . .!" She jerked away to the very tips of his fingers, which like magnets held her pinned to them.

"Why are you afraid of me?" he grated. "Do you think if I am denied my way I shall throw you down the gorge?"

"You look as if you had temper enough for it." Suddenly the situation was absurd, and she knew she had taken too seriously a threat he had meant as a jest. She gave a shaky little laugh. "How silly of me, and ungracious. I am behaving as if I were alone here with Nikos Stephanos. I'm told it's he who wreaks vengeance from the Rock of Helios!"

"And yet you came here to the Rock." His tone of voice was bruising rather than mocking, and still he held her by the fingertips like a slip of metal.

"You came also, *kyrios*."

"There is a saying, *kyria*, that the criminal always returns to the scene of his crime."

The cicadas shrilled and the falls cascaded, and then suddenly a lone bird cried in the sky, and Hebe felt the shock of his words all through her body.

"I am Nikos Stephanos." He let her go, and he inclined his black head in the most mocking of gestures. "I would offer to walk as far as the taverna with you, as I am on my way to the shore, but no doubt you would prefer to walk alone. I shall keep my promise with regard to the icon. *Adio*."

He turned and she watched him stride away through the wild blue sage and the thyme, walking as the ancient gods must have walked, that arrogant head unbowed by the ac-

40

cusations and the possible sin. A tremor ran through Hebe
. . . his long strides had soon widened the distance between
them and it was too late to tell him that it was his icon
which lay halfway down the gorge . . . below the Rock of
Helios.

CHAPTER III

IT was at dinner at the taverna, the evening of Hebe's meeting with the island's mystery man, that she met Daphne Hilton for the first time.

The sun died away and the sky filled slowly with stars, a great silvery drift of them holding Hebe in wonderment upon the veranda at the back of the taverna, with its stone dolphins at either end and its floor of black and white seapebbles. Chairs and tables of cane were set there, and she had decided to dine outdoors in the soft night air.

Lefkes brought a shaded lamp to her table, and the menu. "Mees Lawnay!"

She turned from the trellis of the veranda and her eyes were bemused by the stars. "It's such a lovely night!"

"Indeed." He spread his hands benevolently, as if he had ordered it for her. "The other lady, Madame Hilton, wishes also to dine on the veranda, and I wondered if you would like to sit with her. She has kept to her room during the heat of the day because of a bad headache. She told Maroula she hates flying, it always upsets her, but she was determined to come to Greece. You would be agreeable to her company?"

Hebe hesitated, not really in the mood for someone who might spoil the Greek starlight by discussing her allergy to flying and its attendant aches and pains. Hebe wasn't without sympathy, but she was still suffering, herself, from the shock of her discovery that Nikos Stephanos and the Captain of the *caique* were one and the same man. For no

42

reason, for the night was warm, Hebe felt a shiver run through her; vividly there sprang to mind that moment when he had plucked her from the golden-stoned rock as if she were a sprig of thyme.

Aware that if she sat alone she would keep thinking of that strange encounter, Hebe agreed to share her table with Mrs. Hilton. If they were not compatible then she could always excuse herself at the end of the meal.

Hebe had chosen her own meal by the time she heard the approach of high-heeled shoes and saw her fellow guest step through the slatted doors on to the veranda. Hebe tensed, feeling the initial shyness of meeting someone for the first time, perhaps intensified by her exclusive devotion to her uncle and to Dion. Their loss had made her feel so acutely alone, and she had to make a real effort to greet Daphne Hilton with a smile.

"*Stin yassou.*" The voice had a seductive quality, though the accent was all wrong. Panels of moon-gold chiffon floated around a sheath of silk covering the excellent figure of a brunette of about thirty. She had a striking pale skin and a mouth whose bloom was like that of the poppies up on the hills of Helios.

"Hullo," said Hebe, and she felt young and unworldly in her simple dress with a wide lace collar. In dark navy, with the collar in white, she felt rather nunlike in comparison to the glamorous American woman. She also wondered why someone so attractive was travelling without her husband, and having to make do with the company of a shy English girl.

"I can't really speak Greek at all," said Mrs. Hilton, without surprising Hebe in the least. "I just know one or two words, which is disgraceful of me when I was actually acquainted with a Greek back in Boston. My, they have made the table look nice! Roses, and they look as if they're made of grey velvet at night, don't they? Have you ordered?"

"Yes. I'm having *paté*, then the *souvlaki* –"

"That sounds interesting. What is it?" Perfume wafted from the chiffon and silk as Daphne Hilton took the chair facing Hebe, and there gleamed at her earlobes, and on her hand, moon-shaped emeralds. She might have been dining at a smart hotel in Athens instead of a taverna on a small island in the Ionian, and curiosity stirred through Hebe. It seemed a strange place, this garden of stone, for a woman so worldly to choose for a holiday ... or had she come here with a purpose, as Hebe had done?

"*Souvlaki* is lamb grilled in chunks with onion, tomato, and kidney. They serve it with a delicious gravy, and potatoes if you wish."

"Potatoes! My dear, I wouldn't dream of ruining a figure it has taken me twenty-nine years to perfect." Eyes surrounded by impossibly long lashes studied Hebe, taking obvious note of the fact that she wore as her only ornament a small gold heart on a neck chain, and that her slim hands were ringless. "Look, I just hate being formal. My name is Daphne, and yours ...?"

Hebe told her and awaited the usual surprised reaction at the rarity of her name. "How intriguing. Wasn't Hebe the cupbearer to the gods?" It was said with a smile, but not an unkind one. "This Greek male I knew in Boston always said that my name, Daphne, was Greek. He told me Apollo lusted after her, or words to that effect. In reality he put it in a more poetic way, as these people can, but it kind of makes an American self-conscious, you know, talking in terms that aren't ultra-twentieth-century. You're English, aren't you? Or maybe Irish, with those

44

eyes of green. They glow in the lamplight like a cat's, if you don't mind the description?"

"Not at all." Hebe had to smile. "Do you plan to stay long on the island?"

"My plans rather depend on someone else." A slightly mysterious smile curved the full, red lips. "What about you, honey? Most young Americans would hate to be all alone on holiday, with no one to share the attractions of this place. I'm told the sea is glorious for bathing, though sharks have been spotted on a really hot day. I dread to think what they mean by a really hot day! After living in Boston for three years I've become acclimatized to a cooler zone. I was originally from New York, you know. I was a buyer for a big store there. The man I married was a director on the board . . . Cliff was a deal older than I am, but we were happy enough together. He had a heart attack several months ago and now I'm a widow."

"I'm sorry . . ." Hebe in fact was startled. It seemed as if Petra drew to her stone garden the people who were bereaved.

"Madame!" Lefkes came to Daphne Hilton's side with the menu. "Would you now like to choose your dinner?"

"I guess the *souvlaki* sounds real Greek, except that I'll have mushrooms instead of potatoes."

"I regret, madame, that our soil is too sun-dried for mushrooms, but we can offer you aubergine."

"Fine, I'll go for that, with the fish roe *paté* to start with. And, Lefkes, we must have wine. Not that pine-and-polish you call *retsina*, but a Rhodes wine if you have one?"

"We have whatever you desire, madame." The black moustache quivered with Greek pride, and a touch of humour. "All but the mushrooms . . . the island of Petra has the occasional thunderstorm, but her sunlight is too strong for their growth."

He departed, to return five minutes later with a long-necked bottle wrapped in a snowy napkin, a pair of stemmed glasses, and a saucer on which reposed a few slices of lemon. He uncorked the wine and as if this were a ritual he stroked the rims of the glasses with the lemon before pouring the wine.

"No wonder Greeks are such good actors," laughed Daphne Hilton, after Lefkes had padded away again, with the animal litheness of the Greek male. "They add a touch of the dramatic to everything they do or say. Have you noticed? Or maybe you don't know them all that well just yet?"

"I've noticed." Hebe touched her lips to the wine, and was reminded of her dramatic encounter with Nikos Stephanos. His was a face and a fury out of Greek tragedy itself, but she had no intention of mentioning to Daphne that she had met him. She only wished that she had no need to see him again, but there was still the matter of the icon to settle.

Far out on the dark water as they dined were the lanterns of fishing boats, and they were entertained by some *bouzouki* music while they enjoyed their Turkish coffee. The pulse beat of the music was pagan and irresistible, and though Hebe would have liked to listen in silence to it, the wine had made her companion talkative. She offered her cigarettes, but Hebe didn't smoke, and the flash of the emerald ring was like a firefly flitting about as Daphne fitted a cigarette into a holder and lit it with a tiny gemmed lighter. Her dress, her manners, and her possessions, had about them a sensuous love of luxury; the acquired taste for it of an attractive woman who had set out to capture

46

a man of means, who had probably never cheated him, but who had about her a sort of enjoyment of her wealthy widowhood.

Hebe rather liked her, despite her tendency to talk while the Greek music played in the starlight.

"You're just a little mystifying, aren't you, honey? What brought you to Greece ... tales of how handsome the men are, and still with a touch of the cave about them?"

"No," Hebe protested, but with a smile, her fingers among the petals of the roses which bloomed too quickly in the hot sun of the island and died too soon. "My trip is a sort of pilgrimage, that's all. I wanted to see the country my father helped to fight for."

"What a very British reason. But it's true about the men, but you aren't showing it if you're interested. I believe you're Kipling's walk-alone cat."

"Perhaps." Hebe's smile became enigmatic, which was in keeping with her green eyes and her tawny hair. "I'm beginning to think that it's safer, and less liable to hurt, if you walk alone."

"Running from a broken heart, Hebe?"

"You can't run from one of those, you take it with you."

"So it's that, eh? Did he let you down?"

"No ..." Hebe braced herself to say the cruel words. "He was drowned off a beach we had known together all our lives. He was young and gay and kind ..."

"My poor child!" Daphne Hilton looked genuinely shocked and sympathetic. "How awful for you, and how trite it would be of me to say that time will dull the pain. But it will, and I suppose that in itself is a sort of agony. That inevitably we forget."

"Don't . . . please." Hebe crushed the rose petals, fallen from the flowers that were so lovely only a short time ago. "I never want to forget his face, and the way he had of laughing . . . I know he was laughing when that boom swung and stopped the world from bouncing like a ball in his hand. I know . . ."

"It's fate, honey. The stars write the cheque and we sign it. It's life, half daylight and half darkness." Daphne sat still for several moments, only moving her hand to carry her cigarette holder to her lips. The smoke mingled with the after-tang of wine and Turkish coffee, and the scent of dying roses. "Take that Greek I was telling you about. When I first knew him, he had the world at his feet like a spangled playball. He had breeding, a sort of beauty, and the loveliest bride a man could wish for. He and his young wife always made me think of Scott and Zelda Fitzgerald, somehow. Their glamour and their love seemed indestructible . . . and then fate struck at them and their world turned dark."

Daphne sighed, and the music of the Greek mandolin seemed to match this sudden mood of sadness. Overhead the stars sparkled densely in a sky of pall-velvet. Every scent and every silhouette was so entirely Grecian.

"The Greeks are great fatalists, you know, and I guess the philosophy of that guy rubbed off on me. I always called them Cicely and Chalcous — man of bronze! His eyes were so superbly alive and arrogant. His entire personality had a rare and fabulous quality, such as I had never met in anyone else . . . though I heard he had a cousin named Paul who was equally striking. I guess in old, old families the blood tells, and shows, and creates the kind of thoroughbred who stands out in the crowd. It creates the kind of man who can be incredibly charming and indulgent in some ways, and so savage about things our kind of men take for granted."

"You mean with regard to marriage?" Hebe said quietly.

"Yes. They really believe that a wife is the biblical rib. They really take her as part of themselves, to keep and protect and tolerate, no matter what. And you know Americans! The least little thing and they break up! But for Greeks, especially the couple I'm talking about, it really is a life and death bond. It's joy or tears, and they accept both with a kind of relentlessness . . . but you're young, Hebe, a mere girl, perhaps I'm boring with you with all this soul talk?"

"No," Hebe assured her. "I prefer it to frivolity. Although I loved Dion's laughter, I also enjoyed his intelligence. He made other young men seem futile."

"You'll feel differently one day, when the pain of losing him isn't so raw."

"No," Hebe shook her head, certain with all the certainty of youth, "there could never be another Dion."

"There won't be, honey, but there will be another man. You can't escape it, not with those mysterious green eyes."

"If any man tried to make love to me," Hebe said in a quietly fierce voice, "I'd hate him for it. It would feel like . . . an infidelity."

"My dear . . ." Daphne Hilton sounded rather at a loss, "you are an intense young thing, and I believed British girls so cool, serene and unruffled. You must have some wild Irish blood in your veins."

"My grandmother was from County Kerry, but I don't think my feelings are so unusual. Look at the Greeks . . . you said yourself that they take love very seriously."

"Marriage, honey. A lot of them marry a girl for her

dowry, and it is then a matter of honour to stay faithful even if love isn't part of the bargain. Not all of them marry against the will of their family, as Nikos did –"

"Nikos?" Hebe broke in.

"That Greek friend I was telling you about. The Stephanos clan had it planned that he marry the young sister of Paul, the head of the family. But Nik fell for Cicely while in Boston to take control of the family shipping business in that part of the world. From all accounts the family was stunned when he wired to tell them he had married an American girl, but Paul Stephanos had himself married a lovely Britisher, so there wasn't much he could say except *panta khara*. But sadly things didn't work out happy always for that divine couple –"

"I know," Hebe murmured, "the wife of Nikos Stephanos died from a fall near their Greek villa, and the people of this island whisper that it wasn't an accident."

Daphne stared across at Hebe, whose eyes in the lamplight seemed like those of a young sorceress casting a spell.

"Nik wouldn't harm a hair of Cicely's head! I knew them in Boston. They dined often at our house, and they were perfect together, he so dark, and Cicely so fair. They were a pleasure to look at and to be with. They were aglow with life, infectious with fun –"

"Fun?" Hebe echoed, recalling that aloof and frowning man who had given her passage on his *caique*, and who that morning had bruised her body with his hands. "I can't imagine him ever laughing!"

"Rest assured that he laughed often, during those first few years of his marriage."

"But what drastic thing happened to kill the laughter?"

"Something . . . I don't know . . . he never spoke of it.

50

Then they left Boston and returned to Greece. It came as a shock to hear that Cicely had died. I had been on a cruise, so I didn't get to hear about the tragedy until I returned home. I was so upset for Nik, and for young Ariadne She's six years old, about, and it's always difficult for a man to bring up a daughter on his own. Governesses are no use . . . the child needs a mother!"

It was Hebe's turn to stare at Daphne Hilton, and suddenly it was no longer strange that such a woman of the world should come on a visit to Petra.

She had come to see again the Greek who had so fascinated her in America; the man who was now a widower and free to take a second wife. The attractive Daphne, with her glossy dark hair, and her hatred of aircraft, had flown to this Greek island because she wanted the man who lived in the shadows of an unexplained tragedy . . . whose child had been born in America and was used to the warm drawl and the indulgence towards children of most Americans.

"Have you met him?" Daphne demanded, and a sudden thread of steel seemed to run through the seductive voice.

"Yes . . . he brought me to Petra in his boat." Hebe refrained from mentioning the icon, which had strangely linked her to this man. "I can't quite picture him as you have portrayed him . . . he struck me as statuesque and grave, as if his youth happened long ago. I can't help but feel sorry for the child, shut up in a house without visitors, with a guard at the gates. It must seem like a prison!"

"Perhaps he fears that an accident may happen to Ariadne." Daphne gathered up her gold purse, her cigarette case and her lighter, and rose to her feet. "I plan to see Nik tomorrow, and I might as well admit that I plan to be a guest at the villa. I knew him in the old days, when he was the best-looking guy in the city of Boston; when people turned their heads to watch him enter a theatre or a restaurant. I can't believe that the Nik I knew has turned to a man of stone!' "

She swept away, rather like a queen who had just chastised an impertinent subject. She didn't say goodnight, and Hebe couldn't change her own opinion of Nikos Stephanos. He had struck her as a man who bore a terrible secret

She arose and left the veranda to stroll in the garden, which had steps leading down into it beneath a rustic archway hung with a berry vine. The small bunches of unripe berries swung like silent bells as she walked beneath them, and the stunning smell of pine trees at night was strong in her nostrils. She breathed deeply of the scent, for it was so tangy and so Greek, and the stars blazed down through the pines as they gave so freely of their dusky incense.

It really was a delightful old garden, sunk beneath its rough stone steps. A place to wander with a memory . . . and then as the starlight broke in a flood through the branches of the trees she saw an old stone fountain set in a small grove of wild pear trees. She knew them to be pears because of the twist and droop to the slender branches, the way they bent beneath the burden of leaves and tiny fruits. When she drew near to the fountain she saw that it was fluted like a minaret and carved with deep, strange patterns. It must be Turkish, for the Greeks had never indulged in a display of intricate workmanship. Their art had always been as pure and definite as the profile of a true son of Greece.

Yet she liked the fountain; it seemed so at home in its setting of old biblical trees. It was strange that the Turks had always been less pagan than the Greeks, who had always worshipped Olympian gods and legendary sylphs, making in marble and skin-gleaming bronze figures of such beauty that long, long ago Greek eyes must have seen these divinities and left the memory of them in the very bones of their descendants.

Beauty and torment, she thought. In the eyes and in the landscape of these people who loved the tactile feel of worry beads; whose prayers ended with a kiss upon an icon; whose fury was a torrent rushing down over rocks to send a woman to her knees.

Fascinating, and also fearful, yet here in this old garden Hebe felt a primitive gladness that she had come to Petra . . . strange that here she could feel Dion's presence . . . so tangible that her every nerve responded as a footfall stirred among the twisted olive and pear trees. She swung round and stood tensed against the stone rim of the fountain . . . but the figure that stepped from among the trees was taller than Dion had been, with an aura of power and aloofness. He came to a halt and stared at Hebe, the starlight on her hair making it seem ashen about the pale contours of her face.

"We seem," he spoke abruptly, "to have a habit of meeting in unexpected places. Have you lost yourself this time?"

"No . . . it's such a perfect night that I was taking a stroll before going to my room. I'll go now . . ."

"Wait!" It was a command, not a request. "I came to see you. I have something which you lost this morning."

He held out a small wrapped package and Hebe was reaching for it when she realized that it must be the icon. "So you found someone to fetch it?" She met his eyes, lifting her face to do so and feeling as her hair fell back from her temples rather like a suppliant. It was a feeling she didn't much like. "Is it the icon?"

"Yes, and very beautiful. It would have been a pity to have lost it, and with the aid of a rope I was able to make the climb."

"You?"

"Who else on this island would do so? The Rock of Helios is haunted for most people."

"Isn't it haunted for you?" The words came accusingly from Hebe, despite the vow she had made to herself to remain objective about this man: to stay uninvolved even if her father had been a comrade of his father. But oh, if he had any feelings he would surely find it torturing to go near that tragic place!

"The icon is quite undamaged," he said, without answering her question. "Please take it."

"It belongs to you . . . I came to Petra with the intention of giving it to you, unaware the night you brought me to the island that you were Nikos Stephanos. In the war my father and uncle fought alongside your father, and when they left Greece he gave them the icon. It came eventually into my cousin's possession and when he died I – I thought it should be returned to the household from which it came."

As her words died away, he looked at the package and his fingers slowly clenched on it. "Why did you not tell me this when I told you my name? You let me walk away, and you allowed me to return in search of the icon."

"Y-you went too quickly," she protested. "You gave me no time to explain . . . I didn't think for a moment that you meant to make that climb yourself. I suppose if you had known the icon was yours, you would have left it where it fell?"

"No," he shook his head, "I could not do that. So you mean me to have it, eh? Is it not a memento you wish to keep?"

"It's so very Greek, and my cousin always meant you to have it. I merely acted as bearer and brought it to you."

"Hebe, eh? Cupbearer to the gods?" His dark eyes dwelt on her starlit face, and then he returned the icon to his pocket. "So now your purpose in coming to Petra is achieved? Will you now leave the island?"

She bit her lip and was reluctant to tell him her plans, yet it seemed ungracious when he had risked his neck on her behalf. She met with an effort the eyes that dwelt on her. "I may stay awhile on the island. It's fascinating, so untouched and Greek. I want to get to know the people, to swim in the Ionian, and taste the food of Greece. Do you mind if I stay, *kyrios?*"

"Why should I mind?" A mocking glint appeared in his eyes. "I merely live on the island and have my work here. I don't concern myself with the tourist trade . . . except to rule that my house is out of bounds to sightseers. Some of them might find it a thrill to get a glimpse into the home of a man with a wicked reputation."

"I have not the slightest intention of snooping around your villa," Hebe said indignantly. "Now the icon is in your possession there's no need for us to ever meet again. Good night . . . and good-bye!"

She hastened away from him through the dark garden, and never in her life had she felt such a sense of fury and injustice. He was outrageously arrogant . . . and he was cruel. He had said those things to deliberately hurt her, knowing she wasn't here as a pleasure-seeker.

When Hebe entered her room she found that her entire body was trembling. For most of her life people had been kind to her and now she felt as if someone had come along and struck her for no reason. A sense of forlornness swept over her. It gripped her, held sway over her, but she refused to surrender to it. She wasn't going to be driven from Petra by that ruthless and bitter man. She would stay and suit herself when she left ... and hold to the hope that her path would not cross his stony one again.

She prepared for bed and thrust all thought of him from her mind. And yet in the subtlest way he intruded, for she suddenly started a letter to her parents in Africa, in which she stated that she would be staying in Greece for about a month. At the end of her vacation she would go to London to work for Jolyon Astley, that friend of her uncle's who had an art and auction gallery in New Bond Street. He had been impressed by her interest in paintings and antiques, and her knowledge of them acquired from working as Uncle Dan's secretary when he wrote his books on the subject.

She added in her letter that if the job didn't work out, she would then fly to Africa to join them, and find work there.

Her letter concluded, she sealed and addressed it, and then settled down for the night. She wanted to sleep deeply and not dream that awful dream about Dion, in which she ran all down the cobbled hill by the church, crossing the bridge in frantic haste, only to find when she reached him that he was still and quiet as a figure in marble.

Her eyelids drooped, tension ebbed away, and sleep enclosed her a moment after she heard the call of a night bird beyond her windows. She slept deeply for at least a couple of hours, and then suddenly she was awake again, and everything was very still and very dark. She lay listening to the beat of her heart, and this was not the usual restless awakening, with tears on her cheeks, but one of strange apprehension.

It was as if a voice had called her awake . . . as if a premonition of trouble or danger had crept to her bed-side to whisper a warning.

She drew the sheets up around her, as in her young days when the darkness had scared her, until in a childish treble she had called out to Dion in the adjacent room and he had come in to help laugh away her fears.

Now she was alone . . . and the garden of stone did not invite laughter.

CHAPTER IV

ROCKS and sun-blaze, and a lonely inlet where above in the grass the sound of sheep-bells mingled their soft music with the sea. The caps of the waves were alive and glittering, and Hebe had followed the undulating line of the cliffs until she had spotted this cove and descended a path to its plushy gold sand. She carried a rug and a small basket of food, and wore over her swimsuit a black and white jersey jacket. On her feet were white clog shoes, and she looked carefree, out to enjoy a peaceful bathe and a solitary picnic.

What a morning! She dropped the rug and the basket to the sand, and she stood with the soft wind blowing her hair, watching the waves as they ran liquid and silver towards the shore. The sea, as always, made her think of Dion. He had so loved it, and it might have been fitting that the sea-gods take him, had he not been so young. She sighed, and was glad that it had been swift, and without pain or ravagement.

She turned from gazing at the sea to arrange her rug, to take her book and her sun-glasses from her raffia bag, and to glance in the basket to see what she had for lunch. Everything was just right, and she smiled a little at Daphne Hilton's insistence that young people should desire company. The right company, yes, but Hebe had never been a person to revel in crowds. It was a quiet delight that she had this cove to herself, where she might sit and dream and read, and plunge into that gorgeous water when she felt like it. She didn't care to be chased all over the place by boisterous young men, or to play volley-ball with a giggling group of girls. Hers had always been a reflective nature, with a gaiety that ran deep like a vein of gold. Only a couple of times in her life had she been kissed, and that had been lightheartedly by Dion.

She dropped her jacket to the rug and kicked off her shoes. She walked towards the silvery waves, and wondered what the charming and eager Mrs. Hilton would make of Nikos Stephanos when she met him on Greek soil. Hebe was certain he had changed greatly since he and his wife had been the Bostonian friends of Daphne and her husband.

Hebe stepped over stones into the sea, and then all her thoughts were lost in the delight of treading water until it became deep enough to take her and bounce her on its warm vibrant waves.

She swam and frolicked until she was pleasantly tired, and then as if she were sea-wrack she let herself drift in over the jade swells to the shore. She left her footprints in the sand as she made her way up the beach to where she had laid her rug in the shade of a flowering sea-bush, and where the wind blew cool through a crevice in the cliffs. Now she noticed as she glanced upwards that the rugged walls of rock were the colour of fire and gold, and that the sky above was so intensely blue as to be the holy blue of stained glass in chapel windows. The beauty was wild, with a grandeur to it, and it was hers right now, to enjoy like a gem she could never possess.

Half dry already from the hot sun, except for her wet tangled hair, she slipped her jersey jacket over her swimsuit, and she had a curious conviction that never again would life be so peaceful as it was at this precise moment.

She examined her watch, which she had left safely in her bag, and it was almost noontide . . . the legendary hour of the maenads.

Surrounded by beauty and serenaded by the ocean and the birds, Hebe ate her lunch and poured her coffee from a flask. Maroula had packed the basket and provided her with yoghourt flavoured with fruit, smoked ham and buttered rolls, slices of pink watermelon, and cheesecake. It was good food, made extra tasty by the tang of the sea. The air smelled of wind-cleaned pine trees, which clothed the heights of the cliffs, and of sun-scorched rocks. Her loneliness was a pleasant thing, and her troubled heart felt soothed.

After closing the lunch basket she lay back on the rug and enjoyed drowsily her solitude . . . and her sense of having done the right thing when she had written last night to her parents. The letter had gone to the post that morning and would be carried across the water to the mainland. She was glad she had made up her mind to stay on the island for a while, and she could smile in daylight at the absurdity of her night-time fears. There was no one here who wished her harm . . . there was only Nikos Stephanos who wished her gone.

Well, she would defy him and stay, and if they met on the street she would pass him by as if they were strangers . . . and pleased by the prospect she closed her eyes and proceeded to drift off to sleep with her eyes shielded by her sunglasses and her limbs in the velvety warmth of the sand.

She awoke suddenly, again with a sense of being called. She sat up sharply and looked about her, and it was as if twilight had settled down over the sea and the beach until she snatched off her dark glasses. The atmosphere was hot and still . . . the sea shimmered like metal, and the sands looked primeval. She stood up, as if obeying a sixth sense, and gazed at the sculptured rocks that divided her cove from the adjacent stretch of beach. She thrust her glasses into the pocket of her jacket and walked towards the rocks, gripping them and climbing them with her bare feet, and slithering on the dark beds of seaweed, and feeling the pebbles hard beneath her toes.

While swimming she had noticed the old breakwater that stretched out from the sands and lay like a stone reef that could be walked upon, to where the waves foamed and fretted the end of it.

Right now there was someone out there, a small figure in pea-green shorts, who knelt as if searching the battered stonework for the shellfish that might be clinging to it . . . and there was something else making ripples in the sea, a creature large enough to be seen from the shore, on the prowl around that childish figure who knelt perilously close to the water.

Was it a dolphin? Hebe shielded her eyes with her hand so that she might see more clearly, and what she saw sent her splashing through the rock pools, stubbing her toes and using a few of Dion's cuss words as she made haste to reach that small and foolish figure who had her arms in the water that was being cut into patterns by the jutting fin of a shark.

Hebe had been told by Lefkes at the taverna that sharks sometimes swam inland on a really hot day . . . he had underlined that fact this morning when she had set out for the beach with her picnic basket. "Be careful, *kyria*," he had warned. "If you intend to swim, then watch out for a fin that has the shape of a triangle. If you see such a fin, you will know that it belongs to a shark and you will make haste to swim ashore. Last year a visitor lost a foot, so be careful!"

With these words burning in her mind Hebe hurried along the stone breakwater and she dared not call out in case she startled the child. Here and there the breakwater was patched with seaweed and Hebe was only a couple of yards from her objective when she almost slipped into the sea. A gasp escaped her and the child turned her head at the sound, while her small feet in sand shoes dangled over the edge of the stone.

"Stand up!" Hebe ordered in Greek. "And be careful . . . there is a shark in the water!"

"No." The child shook her head and her dark golden hair glinted in the sunlight. "It's a dolphin, and they don't harm people."

And like a blow it struck Hebe that this incredibly pretty Greek child had been kneeling there, trying to entice to her that finned creature whom she believed to be a playful dolphin. "Come along," Hebe swooped and had hold of the thin young body, "this is no place to play. Come to the beach with me . . ."

"No . . . I want to stay here!" The child struggled wildly, and her huge doe's eyes filled with temper. "I want the dolphin to do tricks . . . I know they can because I've seen them in the big pool in the park at home with Nanna!"

For the second time Hebe received a jolt, for the child had spoken in English without the trace of a Greek accent. And she was tugging so hard to get away from Hebe that the pair of them stood in real danger of toppling into the water, where that menacing fin was still weaving back and forth.

This was not the time or the place for coaxing an obstinate child. and glad that she was not a plump little thing

62

Hebe hoisted her by the waist and to a chorus of yells of protest she made her way carefully along the break-water to the beach, where she took a firmer grip on the young hellion and lugged her up the sands and across the line of rocks to the sheltered cove.

"And now, young lady, you will sit down and eat melon and tell me why you're all on your own, without a respon-sible adult to see that you don't get into mischief."

The child took the slice of melon and sat scowling at it. "I wanted to be on my own, so there!" And again she spoke in English, as if the language were her own, and she gave a wilful toss of her head. "Demi left the side gate open and I crept out, and there'll be holy ructions when he gets found out!"

"Who is Demi, and do eat your *peponi* before all the juice runs away and there's nothing left but the seeds." Hebe also spoke in English and wondered if the child was the naughty offspring of a visitor to the island. It seemed more than possible, if only the child didn't have such huge, brown, beautifully set Greek eyes. They were ex-actly like the eyes of a doe, a little untamed and also strangely appealing.

"He's Demetriades, and he's supposed to make sure that I don't leave the house." Small, even white teeth sank into the pink fruit and juice ran down to the delicate point of her chin. "But I get so fed up with playing in the gar-den and not having any friends. I do like dolphins and I wanted to see one turn a somersault. I did once . . . with Nanna."

"Isn't your nanna with you at the house?" Hebe asked, and she felt intrigued by this precocious child, and rather sorry for her. A big garden and no playmates . . . and she was really only a little thing for all her big talk.

"Nanna lives in America." She spat out a melon seed with the natural delicacy of the Greeks. "I love it there . . and I hate it here, except for the dolphins. Patir showed me one when we came here on his boat. He threw it food and it followed us. Why did you have to come and grab me off that pier? I wasn't afraid of falling into the water. I can swim, so there!"

"I don't think you'd care, my lamb, to be gobbled up by a shark. Don't you know that sharks have a fin like a triangle?" Hebe could feel her heart beating strangely fast as she studied the small girl. She was between six and seven, and she spoke of a grandmother who lived in America, and of a man who guarded the house in which she lived. She was unusually pretty, and Daphne Hilton had said last night that the wife of Nikos Stephanos had been lovely, and he the best-looking man in Boston.

"What is your name?" she asked quietly.

"Ariadne," was the reply. "You're English, aren't you? I can tell by your voice, and you aren't dark like Demi and Zea. She does the cooking for us . . . have you anything else in the basket that you'd like me to eat?"

Hebe had to smile despite the shock of finding herself in charge of the young daughter of Nikos Stephanos. She found a cheesecake and gave it to Ariadne, who had now settled down on the rug, and was eyeing Hebe with a candour both childish and solemn.

"Thank you." She nibbled round the edges of the cake, saving up the moment when she would bite into the delectable squashy part, just as Hebe remembered doing when she was small and curious and full of odd little ways. "Was it truly a shark?"

"Yes . . . whatever would your father do if you were eaten by one of those?"

"I expect he would go out in his boat and catch it," said Ariadne composedly.

"They aren't whales, in which you could catch tiddlers like Jonah."

"Jonah?" The big brown eyes gazed eagerly at Hebe. "Is it a story, and will you tell it to me? Please . . . please!"

"I really should be taking you home, Ariadne. At least as far as your garden gate . . ."

"Please. Nanna used to tell me stories, but no one does any more." The young lips pouted. "I hate this horrible island and I bet if I had some stamps and I wrote to Nanna she would come and take me back to America. It was nice there. I went to school with the Van Carson children and Loela and Regan . . . I wish . . ."

"Of course I'll tell you a story," Hebe said gently, while in her heart a storm raged. Only a man of stone could have dragged this sensitive child from all the familiar things that made a child feel happy and secure. Only an ogre, a dragon could keep her shut up in a strange Greek house that must seem like a fortress to her, without other children to play with, and not even a pet to keep her company. He was cruel and unfeeling . . . hard and hateful. Having punished the mother of Ariadne in some fearful way, he now seemed all set to make his young daughter suffer.

"Well, this is how the story began . . ." Hebe drew the little girl into the protective circle of her arm, and the sea lapped the shore, while overhead the afternoon sky was striped with gold like a tiger's pelt.

Everything seemed at peace, but broodingly. Every now and again a wave would spit and snarl, and the distant mountains had the tinge of iron blue. The sands shimmered hotly, and the cliffs burned fire-gold, and the cool sound of sheep-bells had died away. Not a breeze stirred; the *meltemi* had slunk away and left the sun to scorch the grass and shrivel the white caper among the rocks.

It came suddenly, the tremor that ran like a ripple along the beach, shifting the sands, and lifting the waves into spouts that sank as swiftly as they arose.

Hebe faltered in her story, and Ariadne stared at her as a thrill of alarm passed between them. It couldn't be . . . and yet Hebe had heard of these sudden earth tremors, these heat waves, sometimes no more than a flutter of the pulses, and at other times the prelude to devastation and the loss of lives.

"Ariadne, I think I'd better take you home . . ."

"But the story . . .?"

"I'll finish when we get there." Hebe jumped to her feet and slipped into her shoes. "Now you take the basket while I see to the rug . . ." and there Hebe broke off as another tremor seemed to ripple underground like some great primeval animal stirring in its den. "Hurry, pet. I think we may be in for a bit of a storm and if we show a leg we might just reach your house before your father gets home. We don't want him to be angry with you, not if we can help it."

"Are you afraid of him?" Ariadne gave a giggle as they began to climb the path that led to the headland. "When he frowns his eyebrows join together and his eyes glitter. When he took me away from Nanna she called him a terrible man. Do you think he'll get swallowed up by a whale one day?"

"He'd give the whale indigestion," Hebe had replied, before she realized that she spoke to a child, and that the child belonged to him. "No, Ariadne, there are no whales in Greek waters."

"Look, something big is playing about in the water!" The child paused on the path and pointed to where the sea was sending turbulent waves high up the beach which they had only just left. Hebe looked and felt that clutch of fear, that deep-rooted urge to scurry into hiding from the forces of nature. Had she been alone she would have sought the cover of the pines and waited there among the cool shadows until the earth became calm again, but she was now responsible for Ariadne and must ensure that she reached the villa in safety . . . if it was to be their luck to be kept safe from the awful calamity of an earthquake; to feel only a few unnerving tremors.

"Which way do we go?" she asked, when they reached the top of the cliffs and instinct warned her to get away from them as quickly as possible. If a crack should yawn in them . . . if a tremor should throw the child off her feet . . . a dozen possible horrors chased one after the other through Hebe's mind. "Come, Ariadne, this is no time to pick poppies!"

"You can call me Dee if you like." The child pushed a poppy into the pocket of Hebe's jacket and pointed to a path that ran left, wild as a goat track and probably only used by goats if the villa was so isolated by its position and by order of its master. "This is the way I came to the beach and you'll see our garden and the little temple. I always run past the door because of the stone god . . . he's so cold to touch and his eyes are terribly sad. Zea puts flowers at his feet so he won't weep the house down."

"What an interesting story," said Hebe, hurrying the child even as they talked. "What is he called, your stone god?"

"He's Adonais, and it's funny because that's my

father's second name . . . ooh, I felt one of those wriggles again, right under my feet! I wish to goodness they'd stop!"

"So do I, Dee." Even as Hebe spoke they came in sight of a white wall and a black iron gate, the tall arching sort scrolled into patterns like old lace. Hebe gave a sigh of relief, for this must be the boundary wall of the villa and the rear entrance. Ariadne ran forward and gave the gate a push; it swung open and she turned to grin at Hebe, who noticed when she reached the gate the heavy iron bolt that would be impossible for a child to release. Had it been left unbolted on purpose?

Did someone on the island believe that Nikos Stephanos should be punished for his wife's tragic fall? And did he keep his child in seclusion because he knew . . . but if he knew, would it not be safer and kinder to leave her in America with her grandmother? Anyway, this was not the time for pondering the complex behaviour of the man, and after closing the gate and noticing how brassy the sky over the island had become Hebe followed Ariadne into a eucalyptus grove, where the scent of the tall trees was pungent and the leaves hung like sickles, catching points of threatening sunlight on their blades.

"We're coming to the temple." A small hand clutched hold of Hebe's. "Do you want to look inside?"

"I . . . we really ought to hurry on to the house."

"Only a peep . . . look, there's the little temple!"

The resinous trees gave way to reveal it, solitary and almost haunted-looking, with steps encircling it and the dome above it supported on worn white pillars. Hebe allowed herself to be led up the steps to the entrance, and there she paused to read the Greek inscription deep in the stone: *'One cannot be Greek without suffering.'*

An emotional little shiver ran through Hebe, and then she was within the small temple and there on its bronze base stood the statue of Adonais. She walked closer and gazed up at the chiselled face, ravaged by time and the entrance of the elements, yet with a species of beauty that was eternal and utterly Greek in the shaping of the eyes, the straight line of the nose from the forehead, the enigmatic curve of the lips, the resolution of the chin, the whole fine head on the column of the neck, with a chiselling of rough curls at the nape. The hard lean body was half draped in a Greek robe which fell in carved folds to the tensile feet.

It was a *kouros* . . . a statue of a youth sacrificed to a god. No doubt Helios, the fearful lord of the sun!

"Do you like him?" Ariadne whispered. "Look at Zea's flowers! They're shrivelling up because they didn't want to be plucked."

The asphodels and herbs, and the little wood anemones, were indeed dying at the feet of Adonais, and there was a chill to this place that made Hebe reluctant to linger despite the unutterable attraction of the stone face. "Come along, Dee!" She swung round and involuntarily she cried out, for confronting them in the entrance was the dark figure of the child's father. It was such a shock to see him there, after gazing at the statue, and the glitter of his eyes seemed as ominous as the atmosphere of storm and eruption. It was in fact as if stone had turned suddenly to flesh and bone, with the ability to say things so biting they left their mark for hours afterwards.

In those few shocked moments Hebe felt as if fear scurried across her heart on tiny feet, and the smell of the resinous trees and the sweet decaying flowers seemed stronger. Then a dark lizard scuttled across the mosaic floor of the temple and the movement broke the spell of silence.

"So this time," he said, "it is I who come in search of something lost, and it is you who come to return my errant daughter to me. Well, it repays the debt which you found so hard to bear."

"You could say that." Even as Hebe spoke she could feel Ariadne's sticky fingers clinging tightly to hers, while the thin young body seemed to press close to her as if seeking protection against the hard masculinity of her father. Hebe looked at his black brows and saw they were joined in a single frowning line. Heavens, didn't the man know that a smile could have more effect on a truant child than a dozen angry frowns!

"We've been having a picnic, haven't we, Dee? Down in the cove. Then we felt those tremors and saw the water getting rough, so we decided to call it a day." Hebe looked right at him as she spoke, at the bronze-hard features and the lines which had clawed away his youth and whatever tenderness and gaiety had reposed in him. She could see no sign of the charming and popular person whom Daphne Hilton had spoken about.

"Are you saying that you came to my house – against my orders – and enticed Ariadne to the beach with you?" A flame of anger leapt and burned in his eyes. "When I arrived home from the boatyard I was told that a foreign woman had been here today, but I didn't think you would be so audacious after our conversation last night. I told you then that visitors were not welcome at the Villa Helios!"

"You mustn't blame her!" Ariadne shouted the words at him, and her fingers clenched on Hebe's. "I got out through the gate and went to the beach by myself. I wanted to play down there, and you never take me there, with things to eat."

Abrupt silence followed the childish outburst, and a quick glance at his face showed Hebe the tension of that muscle in his jaw. "The gate was open, small one?"

The child nodded, mutiny on her face and a flicker of terror in her eyes ... accustomed from a toddler to the fair skin and the kindly, lazy drawl of Americans, this Greek parent of hers must seem overpowering in his darkness and his strangeness; his inability to pet and fondle and so make her feel she could trust him with her affection. Instead he inspired terror, and Hebe felt affected in the same way and wished it lay within her power to take Ariadne away from him. A child needed to be loved, not locked up like a small prisoner.

"It would seem that I accuse you unjustly." He said it almost curtly, as if he would prefer her to be in the wrong and at his mercy. "But you must understand that I have given specific orders that all the exits be locked during my hours away from the villa. The cliffs are steep and can be dangerous for a child. Our waters are deep and she is small. I am sure that in taking such precautions I am not being too much the monster, though your eyes tell me I am. What should I do? I have to leave the villa to attend to my business, and Ariadne has a large garden in which to play, and a big attic filled with playthings. There are children in Athens who play in alleyways and have one meal a day, and I would suggest, Miss Lawnay, that if your heart bursts to do good works, you could do no better than to go to the city and commence your duties there."

"Oh ..." Colour flared in her cheeks and she wanted to slap, hard, that bronze and impolite mask of a face. He

71

was truly insufferable . . . . the most arrogant and stony-hearted devil she had ever come across. "I am quite sure, Mr. Stephanos, that you give more attention to your wooden boats than you give to your own flesh and blood. A child who's contented with her surroundings doesn't wander away from them, a child who is given love doesn't seek it from a stranger."

And to prove her words Hebe held up her hand clasped in Ariadne's. "Do you see, *kyrios*? Already your daughter and I are friends."

His answer was an inclination of the head, both ironic and aloof, and implying his disinterest in friendship and the call it made upon the feelings. "As you seem glued to the fingers of Ariadne, which are no doubt as tacky as they are fond, then you had better come to the house."

"No – I don't think I'll impose on your hospitality." Hebe matched his crispness of voice. "I'm sure the burden of being host to an impudent British woman would strain your temper for days to come, and I'd hate your servants and your employees to suffer on my account. Added to which I have quite a walk to the taverna and your Greek earth seems to have the shudders, and if we're in for an upheaval I'd rather like to be dressed for it."

Immediately his eyes raked over her, from her sea-draggled hair to her slim legs below the short hem of her beach jacket. "I returned home earlier than usual because of the tremors, and you might as well know, *kyria*, that our island is subject to them and one of the reasons why it remains free of the tourist invasion. It is called the stone garden because every few years a quake occurs and buildings fall into ruin. It is safer to be on high ground, where the houses are not crowded together, and I can offer you a change of dress as well as dinner. I am sure my daughter

72

would like you to stay. *Ne*, Ariadne?"

"Yes, all night and all tomorrow and next week, too."

And then the most amazing thing happened, Nikos Stephanos broke into a laugh. It was a trifle sardonic, to be sure, but it was a laugh and it made him seem more human.

"Come, you can't deny the child," he said. "Nor can you deny that you are curious about my hermitage. Why not, when you came miles to bring me the icon. You could have sent it to me."

"I wanted to see Greece," she retorted. "I didn't come all this way merely to see you, and I might add . . ."

"You don't have to," he drawled. "You expected the son of a Greek partisan to be equally heroic, and instead you found a man accused of a dark deed. Well, if you are going to sit at that man's table, then you must accept him as you find him. He is what he is."

Enigmatic words which were neither a confession of guilt nor a denial. A statement which was not a plea of innocence, or a defence of wickedness. If she wished to be a guest in his house then she must accept him as she found him . . . mystifying and perhaps dangerous.

"Do you think there is danger of a serious earthquake?" she asked.

He spread his hands in a gesture entirely Greek. "If nature and destiny wish it, then it will happen."

"Everything has gone so still." She looked around her and the leaves of the eucalyptus trees hung without movement, no longer gleaming, because the sky had become overcast. The twisted olive trees were as if enchanted, and the purple oleanders breathed out a dark and secret perfume. "It's a waiting stillness . . . even the cicadas seem to be listening."

'Danger has its fascination ... don't you know that Petra was born of a volcanic eruption from the seabed, which sculptured the cliffs and coloured them like fire? Helios dwelt here and the legend has it that Petra scorned Apollo in favour of the fiercer god, but he was a god without love in his heart."

"Greek legends are always sad and ferocious," she said. "Do any of them end with happiness?"

"What is happiness?" His smile was a brief twist of the lips. "And now let us go to the house. Ariadne, do you wish me to carry you? You are perhaps tired after your adventure on the beach?"

"Only babies are carried and I'm not a bit tired," Ariadne denied, but her feet dragged on the pathway through the garden, which was like the picturesque ruin of past glory, hung with flowers gone wild, with untrimmed vines that clambered over fallen columns and half-broken walls. They mounted some steps and crossed a mosaic pavement, and then it was that Hebe realised that the villa was built upon the site of a far older building, that remnants of it remained, a whisper of old loves and feuds.

They walked beneath an archway that stood on thick old columns, and there stood the house of Nikos Stephanos, white and strong against the dark green of the terraced lemon groves. New to Hebe, and yet not new, for the stone was wind-scarred, the doors and shutters were sun-bleached, and the roofs at varying levels had old curving tiles that overlapped like helmets, and there was shadow deep within the long cloister-like porch. Flowering herbs rambled up the pillars, and a giant cypress lay like a carving against a white wall.

The Villa Helios had a lonely perfection, an immortal look, and looking upwards Hebe saw that one entire veranda was a startling and lovely hanging garden, reached by an iron staircase that spiralled into the air, dark and lacy, lost in a cloud of flowers.

The beauty of the place was unexpected ... and then they entered through the great half-open wooden door, and underfoot was a gleaming black and white stone floor, forming a kind of key pattern at the entrance.

Enter! I am the key of hospitality!

Utterly Greek, like the big pots of plants, with their smooth curves and their primeval patterns. Like the frescoed ceiling, the circular windows, the monastic white inner walls.

The scent of lemon flower ... and the silence ... these were Hebe's welcome into the house where visitors so rarely came.

CHAPTER V

IT was incredible, yet here she was in the house of the man whom she had vowed to avoid in the streets of Petra. Here she was in a bedroom with a vaulted ceiling, white walls, and windows framed by a smooth arch in which hung a lovely antique lamp.

There were steps leading up to the fourposter bed, with the canopy removed so the posts stood tall and dark above the dull gold coverlet. The furniture was simple, but that also was dull gold. There was a certain strange charm to the room, with its single painting of a monk in a medieval hood and habit.

On the dressing-table Hebe saw a mirrored toilet box, and when she opened the double doors of a tall cupboard she was confronted by an array of dresses on hangers, of shoes on trees, of furs in transparent capes. She stared unbelievingly, and then turned slowly to study the door that led presumably into an adjoining room. With abrupt resolve she walked across and tried the handle. It turned and the door opened and the room was almost identical to this one, except that on the dressing-table there were masculine hairbrushes, a leather stud box, a clock in a leather frame, and a belt curled like a snake across a hammered box with silver serpents all over it.

So the change of dress he had offered her was from the wardrobe which still held the clothes belonging to his wife. It seemed shocking, and yet at the same time coldly practical. Why should he throw them out, or give them to charity, or burn them? They were obviously expensive, and Hebe had already formed the impression that he was made of stone!

She closed the door of his room and returned to examine the dresses. Strangely enough Cicely had been her own size, and a fair person fond of pastel colours. An uncontrollable shiver ran through Hebe as she withdrew from the wardrobe a dress of light-blue silk which had many fine pleats that made it hang heavy and rich. It would be like wearing the garment of a ghost . . . her hand shook as she opened a drawer and found a hoard of silken lingerie, some of it as filmy as a cobweb.

It would be a sacrilege to appear downstairs like a shadow of his dead wife! Yet what else could she do, short of sitting down to a formal meal dressed in a bathing suit and a pair of beach clogs? The day had darkened, also, and the sea in the stillness could be heard fretting the cliffs below the villa. Everything but the sea was strangely still, as if some primeval beast waited to spring.

Carrying the light-blue dress across her arm, with fine filmy things, and a pair of silver slippers in her other hand, Hebe walked to the dressing-table and stared into it, lit by gold-shaded lamps on black bases.

Black and gold, she thought. Sunshine and shadow. The tones and the odd appeal of this lonely house. The beauty and the bitterness.

Her eyes looked huge and questioning, reflected in the oval mirror. Her lips were bruised by her teeth, though she hadn't realized she was biting them. What should she do, throw aside these things and flee the Villa Helios before she fell beneath its tragic and its wicked spell? But if she did that, allowed faint heart to overcome her curiosity, and her compassion for the child, then she would be ashamed of herself, as if she had let down the spirit of courage in her father and his twin. That same devil of courage which had burned so gaily in Dion's eyes.

She tilted her chin at a brave angle. "I never knew you, Cicely, but forgive me for intruding and wearing your lovely dress. Believe me, I only want to help Ariadne." She didn't speak the words aloud, for if the spirit of Cicely haunted this room then she would hear them; she would know that Hebe was her friend.

Quickly, because of that adjoining room without a key in the lock, Hebe stripped to her skin and let the silk things slide down over her body. Her skin was clean from the sea, but her hair needed to be well brushed before she arranged it into a thick, soft scroll, which she secured with tiny hairpins from a blue bowl with a tropical bird on it. Her compact was in her bag and she powdered her face, feeling the slight tremor in her hand as she ran the little round puff over the taut, pale-gold smoothness of her face. Her cheeks were faintly hollowed beneath the largeness of her eyes, and her lashes were dark brown and needed no darkening. She took a deep breath for steadiness and ran the pink lip of her lipstick round the contours of her mouth.

There, she was ready if not too willing. A trespasser in another woman's dress! Now she must go downstairs and face a strange evening in the company of Nikos Stephanos, while beyond the walls of his house the forces of nature were restless and the threat of an earthquake was all too real. She had wondered why so few visitors came to Petra; why its rugged beauty was left in its natural state for the islanders to love. Such an island could insinuate itself into the affections, if you were not one of those who demanded every amenity at the touch of a switch.

As Hebe closed the door of the room which had witnessed the love and the fear of a woman unknown to her, she thought of Daphne Hilton, who had been so determined to be a guest at the villa. Instead fate had played one of its ironic tricks and it was Hebe who made her reluctant way down the black, carved stairs to the black and white paved hall where the main rooms were situated.

The hall had the coolness of a cloister within the thick stone walls that bore the brand of the hot sun all day. The circular windows were filled with coloured glass to offset, as well, that daylight glare, and the effect was mystic and the vaulted archways added grace, a sense of being wafted out of time into an age both pagan and aesthetic. Each white and curving arch held something quiet or vivid for the gaze to rest upon. A great vase of deep-toned glass, a Turkish table on short legs with a mosaic top, or a black-figured pot spilling lemon blossom to the tiles.

The scent of the lemon flowers was sweet and unexpected, as if she had expected the perfume to be bitter.

She walked further along the hall and she knew what beckoned her, the flicker of a tiny flame making a shadow against a white wall. It burned in a small alcove, a dense blue flame made by some sort of oil or incense, set alight in a bronze bowl that was studded with uncut stones. Hebe could feel her heart beating rapidly as she gazed at the flame that burned all alone on a white sill . . . it was an eternal light for a lost soul . . . an integral part of a Greek household which mourned the loss of a loved one.

Her hand crushed the silk of the dress she wore, and suddenly she turned to run wildly upstairs, to escape before she saw again the man who was so pagan-hearted that even as he kept burning a flame of love for his wife, he permitted another woman to wear what had belonged to her.

With eyes half-blinded by tears of self-recrimination, she blundered into someone. Hands gripped and steadied her, hard fingertips bruised the bones of her shoulders before relaxing their hold.

She stared upwards through a shimmer of tears into the dark-browed face. "Take your hands off me! I – I can't stay here – I must go and take off this dress!"

"Why?" He shook her and he didn't bother to be gentle. "You are behaving like an hysterical child. The clothes in that room have never been worn . . . the dress is new. All of them, the silks, the furs, the shoes . . . bought in Athens, ordered from the best salon there, despatched too late for them ever to be worn by my wife. Do you hear me?"

She stared at him, and terrible, then, was his look of dark beauty and power.

"They are totally impersonal, without a crease or a mark of face powder. Without a spill of wine or the scorch of a cigarette. Each season a whole new wardrobe was ordered for my wife, because she was lovely and she adored clothes, and I could afford them for her . . . but these . . . these have never been next to her skin. They are as they arrived off the ship, without a whisper of her perfume in their folds."

The words died away and the silence deepened with the shadows, lit in the alcove only by that pure blue flame. It seemed, as Hebe gazed up at him, to burn in the depths of his eyes.

"Do you then believe me such a devil?" he asked.

"W-what else could I think –?"

"You could have had a little faith in me." He spoke with

infinite irony. "There are women who don't mind stepping into the shoes of another – especially if they are silver – but I am not such an insensitive clod that I would take you for one of them. I am inclined to think you too sensitive for your own peace of mind, and I hope I have reassured you with regard to the dress? Have I?"

"I suppose so." She stood taut between his hands, and saw the gleam of onyx at his ice-white cuffs. The immaculate darkness of his dinner suit made him seem taller than ever, and she wondered how long it had been since he had made himself look civilized . . . at least.

"The wicked are often truthful, eh?" A smile flicked across his lips, like lightning before the thunder. "Well, so long as you believe me about the dress, then we can for tonight dismiss your other misgivings. Come, we will go and eat –"

"What of Ariadne?"

"The child fell asleep while I was washing her face and hands, so I put her to bed."

"Truthfully?"

"Yes, I often wash her face."

"You know what I mean! She wanted to stay downstairs and have dinner with . . . us."

"Permit me, *kyria,* to know my daughter better than you know her. She is growing fast and outgrowing her young strength. I brought her to Greece because our air is dry, our sunlight pure and warm. The child will thrive better on Greek soil . . ." As he spoke these words he opened a door, and dangling lamps were alight above the gleam of a dark table set with cutlery and glass, and a bowl of white flowers. The dark rich colours of pictures lit sombrely the white walls. A bracket clock ticked between them, and Hebe took note of the time and was startled. It would be late when she left here . . . very late.

He pulled out a chair for her and she sat down, seeing everything at a glance and being struck by details that made this house and its rooms seem more strangely beautiful than other rooms she had seen. The arms of her chair, for instance, were supported on small golden figures of lions.

Her host walked to the other end of the table and sat down. A little bell stood beside his cutlery and he rang it. "We have few servants," he said, "here at the villa. When I have a guest the young son of my cook does the serving. He may stare at you . . . please don't mind."

"Why should he stare?" she asked, though in her heart she already knew the answer to her question.

"I have few visitors, so you will seem a novelty." He was gazing above her head as he spoke, his eyes upon a wall mural whose sombre colours against the white stone seemed to take on a depth and an intensity that was wholly Greek. "Zea cooks only traditional dishes, so I hope you have developed a liking for the food of Greece, and its wine. It is said of the true Greek that if he has bread, cheese and figs, he is content. We are not a nation of gourmets, and in the olden days meat was only eaten when a lamb had been sacrificed to the gods."

"Do the Greeks still make sacrifices to their gods?" she asked. "I seem to detect in the air of the island a certain paganism."

His eyes looked into hers, and she felt to the depths of her the subtlety of him, and the force, and also the fascination. Such a man might drive a woman to the very edge of despair and yet retain her love, and Hebe was strangely sure that Cicely had never ceased to love him. If they had fought, if they had quarrelled up there by the

Rock of Helios, it had not been over a lover of hers . . . had it been, therefore, over a woman he had wanted?

"Are you unnerved by pagan things, Miss Lawnay?" His eyes held little gleams of mockery, and awareness. He knew she suspected him of having an unholy nature and he was amused by her, as if nothing she believed about him could hurt or irritate him. "Icons, you know, are a form of pagan worship."

"I know," she said. "But superstition and the idolization of false gods is not confined to your island. I'm sure there are those in my country and in the States who kneel before their Bentleys and their Porsches."

His lips gave that little twist of a smile. "You have a sense of humour, perhaps that is why you have the nerve to dine with me tonight. An all too earnest English Miss would surely run from me and my devilish reputation . . . or does my daughter excite your compassion to such an extent that you are prepared to face for her sake whatever torments I may have in store for you?"

"*Kyrios,*" her own smile played uncertainly over her lips, "don't put too great a strain upon my nerves . . . it's enough that an earthquake may be brooding."

"I wonder which would shake you the most, an earthquake or a seduction?"

"I couldn't do much about the first calamity," she retorted, "but I certainly wouldn't sit here a-and be seduced!"

"No, you would not sit there," he drawled, and even as she took in his outrageous remark, he reached with his hand for one of the small white flowers in the table vase and as she watched his fingers seemed about to crush the flower. Instead they fondled, dark against the pallor of the petals, and his gaze dwelt on her face, with its shocked

83

look, and travelled to her slim white neck in the soft opening of the blue dress . . . a dress chosen for his wife who had also been fair and foreign . . . a girl he had married in opposition to the wishes of his powerful family.

"Do you fondly imagine I'd tolerate such a thing?" she flared.

"No, not with fondness." His eyes looked into hers and never had they looked more devilish. "I'd probably have to use force, but your cries would not penetrate far beyond the thick walls of these rooms."

"You're joking, of course!" She laughed, but she knew full well that a girl travelling alone in a strange land had only herself to blame if she landed in trouble, and of her own free will she had walked into his house, so set apart from other houses, high in the stony hills of Petra! She was alone with him but for a couple of servants and a child . . . and it was there in his eyes that he could be ruthless . . . and fascinating.

She was glad when the door opened and a black-haired boy carried in a tray on which stood lovely old soup bowls and a narrow seeded loaf sliced down the middle. The boy stared so persistently at Hebe that the soup was in danger of spilling all over the table, and when he left the room he cast another glance at her, as if to convince himself that he was not seeing a ghost at his master's table.

Hebe tasted her cream soup, which had a subtle lemon flavour. "I believe you enjoy shocking people," she said.

"I believe that people enjoy being shocked." He broke off a hunk of bread and buttered it. "Relax and eat, and stop worrying about my motive in asking you to dine with me. I know you are impatient for the answer, being a woman . . . mmm, excellent soup! But being a man I am going to torment you until after we have eaten. My day is a hard one and I look forward to this hour of peace and good food."

"Why, *kyrios*, do you toil so hard when I have heard . . .?" She paused, for she was being personal and he might resent it.

"You have heard that I belong to a family of power and position, with shipping interests in many parts of the globe. This is quite true. There was a time when I played an active part in the family business, but now I work for myself. I was not dismissed from the family circle, I chose to withdraw, and to design and make *caiques* that would travel strongly and last many years, and also look beautiful. You have seen the *Kara* and sailed aboard her, and she was built by me."

"The *Kara* is beautiful." Hebe spoke sincerely and with a little note of wonderment in her voice; she had not expected him to talk about himself, to reveal that he had a human side to his nature. But of course he had! Ariadne was the living proof that this man had loved a woman with passion and warmth . . . until something, or someone, had caused a rift in their relationship.

"She is named for a cousin of mine," he said, and a moment before he wiped his lips with his napkin a fond smile played there. "We grew up together, and from a rather odd little monkey she grew into a most attractive creature. She married a wild Irishman, but now they are a settled, if far from staid couple, on a thriving furniture-tree plantation in the Caribbean. They had their troubles, one way and another, but now they are happy. Their sons, Terence and Shaun, are rapscallion redheads, which is certainly an innovation into a family as Greek as mine."

Hebe smiled, but she wondered if he ever regretted going against his family's wishes and marrying outside the clan, on the far shores of America. Yet, oddly enough, it seemed a family tendency. Had Daphne not said that his cousin Paul, the powerful head of the family, had married an English girl?

"You are looking at me in a whimsical way," he drawled.

"For proud Greeks you all seem very democratic."

"You mean with regard to marriage, eh? Yes, it has often happened that Stephanos blood has mingled with Anglo-Saxon or Celtic blood. This accounts for the fact that Paul and I are on the tall side. Paul and his wife are wonderful people."

"You love your family yet you . . ." Hebe bit her lip, for scandal clung to his name; doubt and suspicion sat like dark ravens on his rooftop.

"Yet I choose the garden of stone . . . a fitting place for the man without *philotimos*."

"Love of honour," she translated. She looked into his eyes, so very dark, where anything might lurk for the woman drawn into them. They held her, as if they meant to magnetize her, and a pulse beat fast in her throat, leaping as the door opened and the boy arrived with the main course of their meal.

Roast hare, baked vegetables, and a dark gravy with a blissful aroma.

"You will join me in a glass of wine?" he asked, and even as he spoke he was approaching her with the wine jug. He leant over her and she felt his power and his pride, and his danger, as he poured the purple wine into the long-stemmed glass. She felt his glance as it passed over the fairness of her hair, which she had arranged in a Grecian style. Her neck felt bare and vulnerable, and she tautened, as if this dark stranger might suddenly bend his head and brush her skin with his lips.

"Are you afraid of the rumours?" he murmured. "Or are you afraid of me?"

"Of both." She forced a note of flippancy into her voice. "Your wine is like the dark purple seas."

"But it will taste of the warm Grecian nights." He left her to return to his seat, and he raised his glass so the tint of the wine caught the lamplight. "Shall we drink to Fate, the most fickle and unpredictable female of them all?"

"Why not?" said Hebe. "She seems the mistress of us all."

"Quite so. To Fate, *kyria*, who arranges whom we shall meet, to love or hate." He tilted his glass to his lips. "Drink with me!"

It was an order and she obeyed . . . and immediately afterwards she was shocked when he deliberately smashed his glass against the edge of the table.

"Why did you do that?"

"Only because I felt like doing it." He lifted his knife and fork to attack his dinner. "Don't you ever give way to impulse, or does British restraint hold you back?"

"I should hope my impulses are not so dangerously untidy."

"A very British attitude." His smile was subtle, and dense were his eyes, the lashes casting their shadows on to the planes of his striking face. The thought struck Hebe that at the time of his meeting with Cicely he must have been extremely handsome, but like that statue in the little temple he was now weathered by life, and lines almost savagely deep had carved their way into the dark beauty of his face.

"Are Greeks so very different from other people?" she asked, tasting the traditional roast hare of Greece and finding it delicious.

87

"Perhaps so . . . our land is one of savage beauty, where often for miles the soil is too harsh to yield crops or grain; where the olive and the fig tree twist their branches in the sun like martyrs in flames. To be a Greek is to be tough and uncompromising; shrewd and stoical. We are aware that our roots go deep into history, and so we are proud. But even so you must believe that even a Greek has his moments of . . . heart."

"I don't disbelieve it," she said, and she was picturing him with Ariadne, washing the grubby face of his small daughter. How rebellious Ariadne had looked, standing in the shadow of his tallness and looking like him as she defended her new-found friend. Hebe could not suppress a smile. "I hope, some time, that you will allow me to see Ariadne again? Perhaps I could arrange another picnic . . . ?"

"What mischief was she up to when you found her, *kyria*?"

"Oh . . . she was out on the breakwater and I thought it best that she play on the beach. The water was turbulent and I was afraid she might fall in."

"Sometimes a lone shark swims into our bay, and that is one of the reasons why I like the gates secured. I shall have to speak severely to Demetriades, the man I employ for the garden and the groves."

"There was a shark in the bay," Hebe admitted. "When I noticed the child far out on the breakwater I dashed after her. I think Ariadne needs . . ."

"Yes, *kyria*?" He was looking at Hebe with a disturbing directness. "Please go on and tell me what my daughter needs."

"No, it really isn't any of my business . . . except that she seems lonely and has no playmates. Couldn't another child come to the villa to play with her?"

"There are no parents in the village who would care for such an arrangement." He spoke with irony, and tinkled the little bell at his elbow. "Zea will have made a real Greek dessert, so I hope you are not too replete to enjoy it. It will probably come as a surprise to you that Greeks have rather a sweet tooth."

"Why should it surprise me?" She was still shaken that he should admit so openly that the parents of the village did not like their children to play with his child . . . it had stabbed, that remark, for the sake of Ariadne. Must she grow up with a cloud over her young life? If so, then he was being heartless to keep her in Greece. Hebe wanted to tell him so, but she hadn't the right, or the nerve. It could be that he needed the child and hoped to gain her affection, but had he not looked ahead to the time when she would take notice of the rumours and the speculation? She would surely hate him if she believed him to be the murderer of her mother!

The door opened and a stout woman bustled in bearing a large plate on which stood a luscious tart, the open sort filled with fruit and thick creamy custard. Nikos Stephanos introduced his guest to her, and she gave Hebe a searching look. "No, this is not the one who came earlier," she said to him, as she cut generous portions of the fruit tart. "That one had dark hair, lots of paint on her eyes, and big pearls around her throat. A rich one! Kairtes brought her in his cab. They went away in it, and she was not pleased, *kyrios,* that I did not invite her into the house."

Daphne Hilton's name sprang to Hebe's lips, but she bit it back. After all, it was none of her business, and she was sure that Daphne would find a way to see him. She had come a long way, and she was not the type of woman to be discouraged for long.

"We will have our coffee in the *saloni*, Zea. After we have eaten your excellent pastry. The entire meal, as Miss Lawnay will agree, has been *endaxi*."

"You are a wonderful cook," Hebe smiled. "That gravy we had with the hare was like nectar."

Zea slowly smiled in return. "I am pleased, *kyria*, that you enjoy my cooking. I teach all my daughters before they marry, and now they have husbands who would not stray an inch."

Hebe laughed. "We always say in England that the way to a man's heart is through the oven door."

"And we in Greece," Zea shot a look at Nikos Stephanos, "say that even a barbarian is amiable after a good meal."

The silence which followed Zea's departure from the room was not ominous, however. When Hebe dared to glance at her host after several mouthfuls of delectable tart, she found that he was looking at her with a quizzically arched eyebrow. "Zea is loyal to me because she knew me from a boy, if you are curious about that detail. She worked many years for my mother and she came here to Petra with her son when I needed her. She came to the villa for the child's sake . . . as you did. You will stay for coffee?"

"Yes . . . if you wish?"

"It is my wish."

CHAPTER VI

THE *saloni* was a room of oriental charm, with its deep-textured carpets, its divan strewn with cushions, and its Turkish table on legs just high enough to raise it to the level of the divan.

A wind stirred the long silk curtains as they entered, and the chains of the lamps swung and cast shadows over the pale walls. Hebe looked about her, intrigued and yet nervous, and she drew away with the delicacy of a cat as masculine fingers strayed against her shoulder. "The coffee waits to be served." He indicated the silver pot on the table in front of the divan, and the little dark blue cups in saucers edged with silver. "Shall we sit down and make ourselves comfortable?"

"Yes . . ." She glanced around for a chair, but saw only another divan set within an alcove, with a bookcase beside it.

"My 'lazy room' as I call it," drawled her host. "The Turks knew the secret of relaxation, as opposed to the Victorians. Yet even they in the end suffered so much from their rigid ways that they had their Turkish corners. Please sit down and pour my coffee."

She cast him a look and caught the gleam of mockery in his eyes. There was a sensuous quality about this room, and he was so ineffably his own master, with a disturbing power to charm when he chose.

"Come, the coffee will cool off." His hand took her elbow and he led her to the divan; his fingers pressed her skin and warned her not to resist him. She sat down among

91

the cushions and regarded him under her lashes as he strolled round the table to the other side of the divan and lowered his tall frame beside her. Had there not been a hint of a smile in his eyes, then she was sure she would have leapt to her feet and made a dash for the door.

"I like my coffee black, with a spoonful of sugar." His tone of voice was deep, with a dash of the devil in it.

Hebe lifted the pot and poured the coffee with care from the long spout. There arose that delectable aroma of fresh Turkish coffee, whirling night-dark into the cups. It was like a ritual, she thought. The entire meal had seemed to hold an element of suspense . . . as if this were the curtain-raiser to something dramatic. She added sugar to his coffee, and cream and sugar to her own.

"Tell me what you think of my house, *kyria*. Do you find its solitude depressing, and its interior very foreign?"

"I find it has a certain beauty, an air of being divided between modern Greece and the old one. I would almost expect to find a sunken bath set round with columns."

"And you would find one, undamaged apart from the columns, unused since I had bathrooms installed. The water is piped from the hillside springs, and I pay a devilish tax for its use!"

"If Ariadne had a pool," Hebe ventured, "she might not wander off in search of the sea."

"She might drown herself, instead, in the pool. She's an impulsive child, with the ways –"

He broke off, and Hebe found herself filling in the gap in his words. Ariadne might have Greek features, but her inclinations were her mother's. Brought up in America, she was spoiled as Greek children were not.

"Would you like another cup of coffee?" Hebe murmured.

He handed her the cup without speaking and she was aware of his steady gaze as she refilled his cup and added a spoonful of sugar. His eyes remained fixed upon her face as he drank his coffee, and again she had that feeling of being magnetized, like a bird. What did he want? What did he ask of her with those eyes so dark and depthless that their intention could not be read?

"Have you ever felt a wild impulse to do a wild thing?" he asked. "Something that you want to fight against, yet which has a fascination you can't resist?"

Held by his eyes, close to him among cushions, pale-skinned in pale blue beside his darkness, she felt the nervous beat of her heart and wondered if this was how a seduction started. She told herself wildly that if he moved another inch nearer to her, she would throw coffee in his face.

"Your eyes are green as a cornered cat's," he mocked. "Don't be agitated . . . I am not so lonely and distraught that I really need to force a woman into my arms. H'm, while we dined I thought blue your colour, now I don't think so. It doesn't suit your eyes."

"Well, I can't change them to suit your . . . to suit the dress." She bit her lip and lowered her gaze, for it would not be discreet to mention his wife. She, presumably, had been blue-eyed. And her hair would have been truly fair. Hebe had tawny hair . . . she had been Dion's golden cat.

She shivered as Nikos Stephanos placed a forefinger beneath her chin and lifted her face. "Is there someone in England to whom you must return . . . or is there no one? I don't ask merely to pry. I have a reason for my curiosity."

"A reason?" Her eyes ran over his dark features as if seeking it there.

His lip quirked as if he were aware that he had features that were not easily readable. "I had the impression on board the *caique* that you came to Greece to escape from a certain unhappiness, or a sadness. I have therefore wondered if you intend to stay long at Petra."

"For as long as it suits me!" She stiffened and would have jerked herself out of his reach, if he had not suddenly gripped her chin with his fingers, not painfully but insistently. "I told you last night, it isn't any of your affair if I linger at Petra or any other Greek island. You don't give me orders . . ."

"Please simmer down, child." He said it amusedly, as if he were talking to Ariadne. "What a very ready temper you have, and what an imagination. One moment you are certain you are going to be ravished by me, and the next you are assuming that I am telling you to leave the island. Come, lean back against a cushion, relax while I light a cigar." With firm hands he made her recline, pushing behind her head a dark crimson cushion. He then studied the effect. "You have an attraction a little out of the ordinary, so it has to be a man who has made you unhappy. Dion, eh?"

She flinched as from a blow. "How can you know his name?"

He shrugged and turned aside from her to open the cedarwood box that stood on the divan table. "You spoke the name, but perhaps you were not aware that you did so. You slept awhile on my boat, remember? The name was upon your lips as I awoke you, and therefore significant. Perhaps you thought for a moment that I was Dion."

"No!" Hebe could almost have laughed at the idea, had it not been for the bleak sense of loss at the mention of

94

Dion's name. "You and he could not be more unalike. Both physically . . . and in other ways."

"And yet he managed to hurt you in some way." There was in the deep voice a note of irony, a twist to the lips as he applied a light to a thin, dark cigar.

Hebe hesitated, and then decided not to tell him that Dion was no longer alive. "No one can expect life to be all smiles and no scratches, and I'm not a child, *kyrios*. *I* know that life can be frightening at times because one feels hidden forces at work behind the scene, arranging things ahead of our own decisions."

"*Le destin*." He said in French, and blew a perfect smoke ring that wafted up towards the lamps on their softly gleaming chains and dissolved into a small blue cloud. Hebe turned her head against the crimson cushion and gazed silently at his profile, the dark thick hair ruffled at the temples, the deep line that scarred his jaw. He sat close enough to Hebe to be touched, the husband of a young woman who had fulfilled a tragic destiny. People whispered that his wife had died at his hands . . . the lean, strong, precise hands of a man who knew all about boats. Powerful hands, and yet they had fondled a flower.

A shiver ran through Hebe, as if those hands had touched her. Was it from stern pride, or sheer indifference to public opinion that he chose to stay in residence at the villa, among the things Cicely had touched, among the flowers she might have tended, insistent that her child live here with him, isolated from the friendship of other children. The women he had employed to be her governess had not stayed long at the Villa Helios. Had they left because of the talk, or because they found the house a lonely one?

"No, you aren't a child," he said. "But I believe you are

95

young at heart . . . your eyes seem to me as innocent and seeking as the eyes of Ariadne. Did she tell you of the enormous doll's house in her attic, which my partner, Stavros, is gradually filling with furniture which he carves in his spare time? I believe you would not find it trivial . . . no, I am sure you are not a young woman who merely aches to be married."

"What a strange thing to say!" She looked at him wide-eyed when he turned to her and quirked his eyebrow, the outward sign that he was inwardly smiling.

"Strange, eh? Not personal or impertinent?"

"Those as well, I suppose. But it really is true that I have not the faintest inclination to marry. It would seem like prison to me."

"Because of the young man called Dion." It was a statement, not a question. "Do you think this house would feel like a prison for you?"

"What do you mean?" She stared at him as the smoke of his cigar played over his face, losing itself in the grooves and among the planes, and making his eyes seem more mysterious than ever. What could he mean . . . in a short while she would leave his house and return, perhaps, to visit Ariadne if he should feel inclined to permit the visit.

"You said yourself, *kyria,* that my young child is lonely, that she needs company. I agree. She needs someone to walk and talk with. To take her swimming, and to the *patisserie* for ice-cream and cake. To amuse her in general . . . until a governess arrives from America. I made the mistake of putting her in the charge of companion teachers from Athens. I hoped she would forget America when she came to live here, but I did not take into account that half her blood, her personality, her thinking is American. You are not of that country, but you speak the English language, and you are young and the child has taken to you."

"I have taken to her," Hebe said. "Are you saying that I may call on her and take her for walks?"

"I am asking, Miss Lawnay, if you will stay at the villa and be her companion for a while. To keep her company during the day, while I must work. To ensure that she doesn't stray as she did this afternoon."

"I should be only too pleased to come here during the day —"

"No. The arrangement must be that you reside at the villa. That you are here when the child awakes in the morning, and when she goes to bed at night. She needs to feel secure ... unhappily she does not feel secure with me. She needs the care and the company of a woman, and I have decided —"

"*You* have decided?" Hebe felt at once that she must defy him. "I couldn't possibly stay under your roof! I'm not a governess! I am a visitor to Petra, a holidaymaker. There would be a scandal, and surely you ..."

"Can have nothing left to be implied."

"I am talking about myself!" She pushed at the Turkish table and leapt to her feet; she stood poised for flight and the next instant was running across the room to the door. She was there, but he was swift, supple as a tiger in pursuit of her, and it was his hand which reached and held the handle.

"I want to leave," she said stormily. "You have no right to keep me here!"

"Don't be agitated." He gave a throaty little laugh. "You know you can't leave unless I let you go. You hardly know the way to the front door, let alone to the village in the dark."

"You're a devil!" she accused. "You're all the things people say about you, and more!"

"Is it so terrible to ask a young woman to act as paid companion to a child? Is it because Ariadne is my child? Would you react this way if it were not Nikos Stephanos who offered you the position?"

"I am not in the market for a job," she retorted. "I am merely here for a holiday, a few weeks of relaxation, and then I return to London to take up a career. What sort of an era do you live in, *kyrios*? You behave as if women are slaves and chattels!"

"Don't be absurd." He said it lazily, but the glint in his eyes set her nerves tingling. "You are not an indolent young woman who likes to be idle, and I don't ask you to make a career of nursemaid and companion. You showed some concern for Ariadne, and it is true that she is lonely. Won't you forget that she is part of me, and remember only that she has a need for a friend? She is a pretty thing, and affectionate. And the villa is quite a pleasant place . . . I am not here for the best part of the day. My boatbuilding yard is down on the quay."

"Don't try and bribe me." She drew away from him in the pale silk of her borrowed dress; from his darkness of hair and eyes and possible intention. He was like an assault on her sensitivity. He was not gallant like the men of her family . . . he was a pagan, self-willed Greek.

"Y-you can't bear not to get your own way." She spoke with a quiet intensity. "It's written all over you."

"You are singularly innocent if you suppose that other men are any different." There was more iron than irony in his voice this time. "Yes, I like to have my own way, but not out of sheer obstinacy, or because I want to bully you. I know my idea to be a good one, the ideal solution until I am able to place Ariadne in the care of an American woman –"

"That shouldn't be at all difficult," Hebe broke in. "It could be arranged tomorrow. A friend of yours from America is staying at the taverna . . . a Mrs. Hilton."

"Daphne?" Something blazed into life in his eyes, then they narrowed to a stony brilliance that was like a wall cutting Hebe off from his personal feelings. "As I have said before, Miss Lawnay, I admire your sense of humour, but don't let it run away with you. A rich and worldly woman such as Mrs. Hilton would not be suitable as the companion of a child."

"Only a poor and unworldly one is suitable, I take it?" Hebe made no attempt to keep the flippant note out of her voice; it was almost as if she invited him to slap her. She knew he was capable of it, and she wanted, almost desperately, a valid reason for not giving in to the appeal of this man's child, this man's house . . . she wanted to be wilful and deny the need of her contained within that young body that sprang from his strange, tragically ended love.

The room was utterly still, and it was a stillness reflected by his face and his entire body. Then, shockingly, the high walls of the room seemed to shudder like living tissue, and the windows shook so hard that the glass seemed about to break. The lamps swayed back and forth and the light spun madly . . . suddenly a mirror fell with a crash and as it splintered and the shards leapt in Hebe's direction, a pair of arms swept her off her feet and Nikos Stephanos was striding with her from the *saloni* as the door blew open in a gust of strong, screaming wind.

"I . . . I felt the earth shaking," Hebe gasped, and it was as shattering as the fallen mirror, the swift transition from terse words to the hard holding of his arms, carrying her swiftly to the arching stone groyne beneath the stairs.

He dropped her to her feet. "I must fetch the child from her room. Stay here and you will be quite safe."

He was gone, racing up the stairs, and suddenly the lights went out and the entire villa seemed to be shifting on its foundations. Tiles could be heard slithering to the stones of the courtyard, and a pair of shutters made a chattering sound, like the big wings of a trapped bat.

Hebe leaned against the stone wall of the groyne in order not to be shaken off her feet by that strange lurching of the earth. She felt a fear of the primitive and the unpredictable racing through her veins . . . the quake had come with swift temper to ravish the island and leave it broken.

She heard footsteps and voices, and saw a candle-flame making a halo around a large madonna-like face. "Zea?" she cried out.

"*Ne, kyria.* Zea and Alik they come to join you. The saints preserve us, but I swear every roof tile is flying off to pave the ground!" Zea loomed beneath the stone shelter under the stairs, followed by her son, who carried a pair of flaming candles like a votive offering.

"And where is *he*?" Zea demanded. "Where is the little one?"

"The *kyrios* has gone to fetch her." Something else broke with a crash and dust blew across the hall. "How long do they last, for heaven's sake?"

"Two minutes . . . two hours. One can't say. Hold still those candles, Alik!"

"Hold still the house, my mother." He gave a choked laugh. "The floor she is dancing, do you feel it, Mees?"

"Yes, isn't it weird?" Hebe could feel her fingertips bruising against the wall, as if like a gnat she clung there for support. Her heart was thudding . . . her nerves were crying out. "Hurry . . . do hurry. The house might fall in . . ." And her mind held a vision of a man fallen in the dust and the ruin, with a dark-haired, pretty child lifeless in his arms.

Then she heard Ariadne crying, and as her father rounded the bend of the stairs into the groyne, the candle-flames leapt and the child hung upon him as upon a cross. Something had struck his cheek, and the blood clung there like a dark teardrop.

"She would not come without her doll, and we had to search for it in the dark. Come, Dee, you can stop crying. Our lighting system is damaged and this is only a sort of game."

By the light of the candles Hebe could see tears trembling in the doe-like eyes, while the small body trembled in the strong arms of Nikos Stephanos. The doll was clutched in one hand, while the other clung to the side of his neck. "M-my bed was dancing," said the child in a voice which still held terror. "A-and the shutters banged, and I wanted Nanna!"

"It is but a storm, little one. It will soon pass, and Alik will play for us and make music so we shan't hear the noises. See, he has brought along his *bouzouki*."

Ariadne turned her head and gazed with solemn wet eyes at the boy who had a wild young grace like her own; the heritage of Grecian youth. "Will you play?" she asked him.

"With pleasure." He smiled and his fingers ran over the

strings of the Greek mandolin, making a trickle of silvery sound which turned in a moment to lively, evocative dance music.

It was the strangest hour of Hebe's life, sheltering with Greeks beneath an arch of stone while the earth shook and down in the village of flat-roofed old houses, built close together, destruction could be happening. She thought of Daphne Hilton, who was accustomed to an easy, smooth life. She looked at the face of the man whom Daphne had come so far to see, and Hebe wondered if that cleft of anxiety between his brows was for the woman he had known in Boston.

Abruptly his eyes met Hebe's, and his face was closed to her, as if all the muscles were of iron. He was like Greece itself, she thought. He was harshly beautiful, elemental and rather cruel. He was also endowed with deep passions that Hebe glimpsed in his Grecian eyes and in the sculpturing of his lips. Suddenly the doll fell from his daughter's hand and Hebe bent down to pick it up. The childish head drooped softly dark against the iron darkness of his hair, and Hebe's fingers clenched on the costume of the doll. For a brief, almost shocking moment, as if she glanced into a private room, she saw a raw blaze of love in a man's eyes for what was part of him, born because of him.

Everything lurched and she leaned back against the stone wall, into the curve of the groyne, as if she would conceal herself from his eyes and what she had seen in them. She had wanted to believe that Nikos Stephanos was invulnerable to human feeling, but now she was forced to admit that he was probably the most passionate and lonely and haunted man she had ever known, or ever would know. She had dared to question his right to

Ariadne . . . he had every right under the hot and powerful sun of his land. He was the child's father. He was Greek and possessive. He would hold and keep her, for she sprang from his strong body and bones, and her prettiness was as Grecian as the asphodel.

Hebe held the doll in its flounced petticoats and its dress of pink lace. The hair was blonde and there were tiny shoes upon the feet. It was a very smart doll, probably given to Ariadne by her American grandmother, and she loved it. And just as the grandmother had given the child the doll, Nikos Stephanos desired to give her the companionship of the British girl to whom she had responded.

He meant to have his own way, just as if she were another doll with fair hair for the child to play with!

The *bouzouki* music played on in a silence none of them were fully aware of, until Zea interrupted the music and the silence with her down-to-earth voice. "I think, *kyrios*, that it is over!"

Alik stopped playing and all of them listened . . . the stillness was uncanny, as if the island lay dead beyond the thick walls of the villa. The calmness was unbelievable after the crashing of tiles, the banging of shutters, the creaks and groans of a house which some primeval thing had tried to tear down. When daylight came the full damage would be revealed, but right now it was enough that the roof was intact but for some of its tiles, and they could brush away the dust from the plaster which had fallen.

Zea crossed herself, even as a candle guttered and the smoke stung the air. "It feels good to be alive, but I think for some it must have been bad."

"If there is enough crockery left intact, then I think some hot strong coffee would do us good," said Nikos

Stephanos. "Alik, fetch lamps and we will take a look at the upper rooms to ensure they can be slept in. Miss Lawnay, perhaps if I take Ariadne to the *saloni* you will give an eye to her?"

"I should be glad to." The relief of being able to walk across the hall without fear of the ground quaking was enormous, and Ariadne slept on in the arms of her father, only stirring slightly when he placed her upon the divan, where earlier Hebe and he had enjoyed coffee and he had asked – no, demanded that she become Ariadne's companion.

He looked at her and she knew he was reading her thoughts. "You will have to stay the night with us," he said. "There is no telling what has happened down in the village, and the rooms here are comparatively unharmed."

"I – I suppose it would be best," she agreed. "It must be very late and as you say anything could have happened."

"Yes, and now I will see about a bed for you." He paused a moment to gaze down at Ariadne, then he swung on his heel and walked from the *saloni*. After he had left and closed the door, and everything was silent and dim but for the flicker of the candle in the stick which Zea had given her, Hebe could still recall each feature of his face, each haunting shadow and angle. There was nothing else for her to do but to stay the night in his house, but she devoutly hoped that he would not expect her to sleep in that room which adjoined his own. It had a communicating door, and never in her life had she felt so uncertain of a man. He was like his eyes, so deep and dangerous that she was out of her depths. He was a law unto himself up here in the wild hills of Petra, and her belongings and the people she could trust were down in the village, which the earthquake could have destroyed in a moment of time.

She studied Ariadne's sleeping face against the same deep crimson silk which had cushioned her own head when Nikos Stephanos studied her. She saw again in the small features an unmistakable likeness to the man, because the dark and the strong impressed their image with more effect than the fair and the sensitive.

Pale blue had been Cicely's colour, an indication that she had not been assertive. Had her fair appeal gradually lessened for her Greek husband, until he had looked elsewhere, demanding a fiercer love, a more clamorous passion, in a woman bold and dusky-haired?

Hebe envisioned Daphne Hilton, who had married an older man for position and money, and whose unused feelings might well have been aroused by a vital Greek with a striking face.

Had they planned to meet again when they were both free?

Seated there beside Cicely's child, Hebe had the most intolerable recoil from the very thought of such a plan. It was hateful, and yet as insidious as the bite of a viper spreading its venom through her system. There had been that instant blaze in his eyes at the mention of Daphne's presence on the island. There had been that brooding look of anxiety on his face during the earthquake. And he had said explicitly that he would not expect so worldly a woman to be the companion of a child.

Such a woman was made to be the companion of a man ... and it was then, in the midst of such reflections about him, that he returned to the *saloni*. He carried a lamp and there was plaster dust on the sleeve of his dinner jacket, and the scratch on his cheek was quite deep, as if he had been cut by a piece of flying glass.

105

"I regret that Zea cannot make coffee. She uses the electric stove only these days, so fuel for the fire stove is not available. We will have a brandy instead, and then you must go to bed."

He placed the lamp on a table and went to the cabinet that stood in a recess. He opened it and took from it a pair of brandy bowls and a slim-necked bottle. "This will settle your nerves. I noticed what a start you gave when I entered the room just now. You are fatigued and you are still shaken."

It was true, she felt weary in every limb and nerve. "I have never experienced an earthquake before. I do hope the people of the village have not suffered too badly."

"I endorse your hope, *kyria*." He came towards her with the glasses cupped in his hands. "I should like to go and make certain that the damage to life and property has not been too severe, but the wrath of the thing might not yet be fully extinguished and I cannot leave two women and a child in the care of a boy."

"Do you mean . . . it might return?" Hebe took the glass he offered and held it in both her hands as if she feared to drop it.

"Yes, the tremors could begin again, so I must wait until daylight to go and see . . . please, drink your brandy. Your hands are unsteady."

She obeyed him, bending her head to the glass so he wouldn't see the look in her eyes. He could hardly be anxious about the islanders, who treated him like an outcast and scorned his child, therefore his worry was for Daphne.

Hebe sipped the fiery brandy and felt it to her very fingertips. She watched him under her lashes as he paced the oriental carpet in front of the divan. His pacing was soundless, like that of a leashed animal who longed to break its chain. Suddenly he lifted his glass and swallowed his brandy without a flinch.

"Drink up and come with me," he ordered, leaning over Ariadne and lifting her with care into his arms. "A room has been prepared for you."

"I – I could sleep down here," she said. "The divan is quite comfortable."

He looked at her, with mockery agleam behind the heavy lids of his eyes. "A bed is much more so, and I am not in the mood to be argued with. I am, *kyria*, quite capable of treating you like Ariadne. Which means that I would not hesitate to put you to bed like a child. Come, you are rocking on your feet and incapable of fighting me any more tonight. Bring the lamp, if you please!"

So, defeated by all that rampant male strength, all that Greek obstinacy, Hebe picked up the lamp and followed him from the room. They went upstairs and along the gallery, and to her unspeakable relief he paused outside a door that opened to reveal a cool, pale room like a sanctuary, with no dull gold furniture or monk-like figure on the wall. The bed was covered serenely in white, and the lamplight flickered on an icon.

"Good night, Miss Lawnay." His eyes held hers for a taunting moment. "Sleep well and don't worry about the earthquake. If it returns, hurry downstairs to our place of shelter."

"Good night, Mr. Stephanos." She hesitated, and then had to give in to what was driving her. She leaned forward and kissed the soft cheek of the child in his arms. Then hurriedly she turned away from him and entered her bedroom. "Good night," she said again, and closed the door.

CHAPTER VII

HEBE slept so deeply it was as if she had been drugged. When she awoke, suddenly, in a strange bed whose covers she had hardly disturbed in her sleep, it was to a blaze of sunlight on pale walls, broken into patterns by the scrolled iron of the veranda and the vines that rambled there in flower.

She lay in a sort of sleepy daze, staring at the sun-made patterns, trying to recall where she was and why she had a curious sensation of having passed through an earth-shaking experience. Had she dreamed . . . no, her sleep had been profound and without a dream she could remember. She allowed her gaze to roam around the room and as her eyes settled on the enamelled icon attached to the wall, the events of last night came flooding back.

Of course . . . she sat up and the covers slipped away from her slender figure clad in a silk garment not her own. There had been an earthquake, and following the alarm and the tumult she had stayed the night at the Villa Helios.

Well, now it was morning and she would be on her way back to the taverna. She got out of bed and the warmth of the sun touched her bare feet as she stood and looked around for her clothes. Her gaze settled upon a suitcase on a stool, and beside it the companion case. She couldn't believe they were hers, but they were, and a mixture of amazement and fury propelled her towards them. The last time she had seen them, they had been unpacked and in her bedroom cupboard at the Firefly Taverna. She opened the one on the stool and there lay her clothes in neat layers, and she knew . . . she knew in a flaming instant who had had the gall to have her things packed and brought to the villa. There was only one person who would be so presumptuous, and never had Hebe dressed so quickly in order to find a man. She couldn't wait to tell him that she had no intention of working for him.

She was buttoning her blouse when all at once there was a tapping noise on her door. She marched over to it and swept it open. Ariadne stood there looking up at her, and there was glee in her doe-shaped eyes. "Zea said I wasn't to worry you, but I knew you'd be awake. I knew you'd be dressed!"

The child came prancing into the room and with the unerring instinct of female curiosity she made for Hebe's open suitcase and peered into it. She touched the things which Hebe had disarranged in her search for a plain white blouse and a pair of slim-legged slacks. She had wanted to look as British as possible, and as far removed from the Greek idea of a governess as she could make herself.

"Have you something you don't want that I can have?" Ariadne wheedled.

Hebe had to smile. "Let me see," she opened the small box in which she kept oddments of jewellery and took from it the little sea-horse brooch which she had worn as a schoolgirl and kept for luck. She wanted Ariadne to have a small token to remember her by, when she left Petra, and the presumption of Nikos Stephanos made her want to leave this very day!

"Here you are, Dee." She pinned it to the child's red dress. "You seem to have a fondness for sea creatures and this is pretty. It's silver, and the eyes are beryls."

"They're green like yours." Ariadne looked down at

herself with a smile of importance. "Can I keep him always?"

"Yes, he's yours." Hebe gazed down at Ariadne, whose hair was tied in a pair of pony-tails with ribbon to match the colour of her dress. "Does Zea wash and dress you in the mornings, Dee?"

"No, I do it myself, but Patir brushes my hair before he goes to work and bunches it for me. Sometimes he does it too tightly and it hurts my eyebrows." Ariadne gazed up at Hebe with eyes like big pools in which sunlight danced; she was extremely pretty, with already a Greek shapeliness to her bones. She had intrinsic beauty which would increase as she grew up, and much as Hebe resented Nikos Stephanos she couldn't help but like his child. She was the better part of him, the distilling of sheer beauty from that hard and pagan frame of his.

"Are you going to stay with us like that other lady?"

"What other lady?"

"The one in the big guest room." Ariadne looked around her. "I like this room much better. I like all the little drawers in the dressing-table, and the veranda is full of flowers. Come and look!"

Ariadne caught at Hebe's hand, but she stood her ground and asked again about this mysterious lady.

"She was crying when Patir brought her home with him, and she had on a fur coat over a long silk dress."

"Crying, Dee?"

"Yes, because the storm broke all the walls of the taverna. Alik told me so. He said a lot of people lost their houses and the lady had to come to our house because she had nowhere else to go."

"I – see." Hebe allowed herself to be pulled between the half-open shutters on to the veranda, which was just

110

like a hanging garden. Absently she admired the flowers, while her thoughts were busy with the unexpected. So he had brought Daphne back to the villa with him, along with Hebe's suitcases. Now he had a legitimate reason for keeping both of them here ... at least, Daphne would want to stay. Her reaction would not be one of panic, and that was the feeling racing through Hebe at the moment.

The taverna had been badly damaged by the earthquake ... she couldn't return there, and was more or less trapped into staying here for the time being. Suddenly she felt almost as shaken as last night, and she was scared ... afraid of becoming involved in the lives of those at the villa. She didn't want to suffer again the pain of wrenched emotions; of feelings laid bare and aching. She had run from England seeking a place of peace in which to lick her wounds ... instead she had run into a storm, and into a house of secrets.

"Dee," she forced a smile to her lips, "I'm starving and would love some breakfast. Have you had yours?"

"Hours and hours ago. Patir told Zea that you were to be left asleep because of all the upset last night. He said you were little more than an English child." Ariadne giggled and fingered the pearl button that fastened the cuff of Hebe's blouse. "Isn't he funny to call you a child when you don't go to school any more? But I suppose it's because he's quite old himself."

"He isn't quite a bearded patriarch," Hebe said dryly, "no more than I'm a schoolgirl. However, we'll let it pass for now and you can show me the way to the kitchen. I'm ravenous for fried eggs and toast, and I can cook them myself if Zea is busy."

"We can go this way if you like?" Ariadne ran to the iron stairs that curled from among the flowering vines to the courtyard below. "You will stay and play with me, won't you? You won't go away when you've had your breakfast?"

"At present, Dee, I've nowhere to go and so I shall have to stay a while, until I can arrange something." Hebe followed the dancing red shoes down the stairs to the paved court that wended its way to the rear of the villa. They had to walk carefully, for the ground was still peppered with broken tiles, and suddenly she glanced up and saw the master of the house straddling a rooftop. She felt the dark shock of his eyes as they met hers, and then he inclined his head in a half-mocking way. "You had a good night's sleep, *kyria*?" he called down to her.

Ariadne skipped about among the fallen tiles, excitedly. "She's going to have breakfast and she's going to stay."

"I understand, *kyrios*, that the taverna and other houses were badly knocked about last night?" Hebe stood shading her eyes from the sun as she gazed up at him. "I hope the occupants weren't badly hurt?"

"There were a few people injured, and I was told that a child was born during the midst of the quake." Teeth flashed white and strong against the dark face of Nikos Stephanos. "It was a boy. He will have quite a tale to tell the girls when he grows up. I understand that the mother is calling him Zeus."

"Zeus?" Hebe gasped at the audacious name, and then she had to smile and admit that it was appropriate. He was the god of elemental things. "I shall have to look around for another inn –" she began.

"We will discuss that matter later on." He stood above her on the rooftop, tall and dark as a storm god himself, intent on shaping events to suit his own inclinations. Hebe

112

cast a glance at Ariadne in her red dress and shoes, like some imp of the fairy woods, and she felt a treacherous weakening of her resolve to stay uninvolved . . . she, who had known the glorious kinship of Dion during her childhood, could hardly bear to deny the child for the sake of opposing the man. Her heart gave a twist in her breast as Ariadne twined a hand in hers and looked at her with the trustful eyes of a young fawn.

The fawn she could cope with . . . but the stag of a father set her nerves on edge each time he came near her.

No, she wouldn't decide here and now! She wouldn't give in to the demand in those down-gazing eyes, darkly burning in that pagan face. He was pagan, she knew it, and such people lived by codes that were unconventional and unpredictable. Poor Cicely had learned this, and she had suffered for it.

"You had better go and have your breakfast or it will soon be lunchtime," he called down, a soft jeer in his voice, as if he knew that he had her half bent to his will already.

"Let's go, Dee!" They ran away from him, and the child was giggling and in rare high spirits when they entered the big, stoned kitchen, with its ceiling beams hung with strings of vegetables and herbs; hams and peppers. There were two big stoves, one of them electric and looking very out of place in this fine old-world kitchen. Copper pots and pans were lined up on shelves, the table and floor were well scrubbed, and though a refrigerator stood in a corner, Zea had not discarded the earthenware water pitchers but made use of them for cream and cheese. It was Ariadne who lifted the muslin covers so that Hebe could see and smell the ripening cheese and the rich cream.

"What a gorgeous kitchen!" Hebe was filled with innate

delight in old and worthwhile things. She knew that one had to be a realist up to a point, but it gave her a sense of warm satisfaction to gaze at those strong beams that arcaded the ceiling, and the red-gold glow of the copperware. In smaller earthenware pots stood red and mauve flowering plants.

It was altogether a beautiful room, the sort she would have liked to paint had she been an artist. Dion had once said that she had an artistic soul and would see beauty not in surface things but always in the heart of the object, whether it be a tree, a house, or a face. He had kissed her left eyebrow after paying her the tribute, and memory was mingled in the little sigh she gave as she gazed around Zea's abode.

Alik poked his head around the door. "The mother is making beds," he announced. "Is there anything I can do for you, mees?"

"Yes, you can show me where your mother keeps the eggs and bread, and the coffee."

"Ah, you are going to cook?" The boy grinned as he opened a deep-shelved larder, as if like all the males of this island he believed that foreign women were ornamental but useless.

"Yes," she said crisply. "You had better ask the *kyrios* if he would like a cup of coffee. I noticed he was busy on the roof."

"If I were a man of means," Alik said impudently, "you would not find me so inclined to work. It is Turkish coffee, not the sort in jars that mixes like cocoa."

"You mean I have to grind it," she said. "Then show me the grinder and I'll manage without the vapours."

He laughed as he arranged things for her on the table. Ariadne had found some cherries and was busy eating the

114

single ones and hanging the double ones over her ears. The sun struck bright through a window and Hebe was amazed by the silky calm of the morning after the upheaval of last night. In daylight it seemed like a strange and frightening dream.

"Perhaps the guest of the *kyrios* would also like some coffee." She tried the electric stove as Alik powdered the coffee beans. Greek males seemed to develop early as dominant know-betters! The power had been restored to the household generator, and she had a vision of the furious activity of Nikos Stephanos since the first glimmers of dawn. It seemed as if the man was driven to hard work in order to exhaust himself physically and mentally . . . Hebe turned abruptly to Alik. "Has the *kyrios* had any breakfast?" she asked.

"I believe not," said the boy. "After attending to the generator he went straight to the village, and after returning with the American lady he started to work on the roof."

"Men are fools," Hebe muttered. "Alik, go and tell him that I am cooking eggs and bacon for him . . . there is plenty!" She gestured to where the legs of ham and sides of bacon hung from the beams. "He can't do all that work on an empty stomach."

Alik gaped at her, as if it were not the custom in this house to show concern for the master of it. Then with a shrug he loped off to do her bidding.

Ariadne, hung with cherries and juicy-lipped, gave Hebe a wide smile. "I think I'll have an egg," she said.

"You have had enough to eat, young lady." Hebe stood on a chair and reached for a lump of bacon. She hoped Zea wouldn't mind this invasion of her kitchen . . . in the oddest way she was enjoying herself. It was a relief, she

115

supposed, after the tension of those hours when it had seemed as if this house might collapse and its stone walls bury her with Greek strangers.

Strangers? She paused in her slicing of the bacon, and then resumed, cutting the smoky bacon good and thick. You couldn't face danger with people and call them strangers any more. She broke eggs into sizzling fat, and laid rashers in the big fellow pan. She breathed the aroma of the bubbling coffee . . . these things were good, and the sun was shining. For now, for a while, the shadows over the Villa Helios were held at bay.

Suddenly a long shadow slanted through the open doorway. Hebe glanced up from the pans. "How do you like your eggs?" she asked.

He entered and water still dripped in small globules from his black hair. He had evidently washed himself at the wall fountain in the courtyard. "Turned on their faces," he said, and he stood there tall and dark, his gaze going from Hebe to his cherry-hung child. "It's good of you to cook for me."

"Zea is busy upstairs, and Alik said you went off this morning without anything to eat. I hope Mrs. Hilton was not too shaken up?"

"She was glad to accept my hospitality, which is more than I can say of a certain other visitor to Petra. Ariadne *mou*, don't keep hopping from one foot to the other like a demented blackbird. Leave the room if you must."

"I must," she dashed past him, "but I'll be back. Don't go away, Hebe!"

Hebe gave a laugh, and shot a look at Ariadne's father. He lounged against the table and she noticed that he had not yet found time to have a shave. With his damp and ruffled hair, his dark chin and his half-buttoned shirt, he

116

looked very different from the personage who had wined and dined her the evening before.

"You slept well?" he asked.

"Like a log. What was it you gave me to drink . . . the devil's nightcap?"

"It might have been." He rasped a thumb down his lean jaw. "In reality you had an overdose of excitement."

"The kind I can do without." She dished up the eggs and bacon, and was reminded of the meal she had cooked for him on board the *caique*. "I don't like it when people are hurt and lose their homes. I – I suppose I'm soft."

"Do you imagine I was unmoved by the sight of wrecked homes and women with tears in their eyes?"

"No –" She thought of Daphne with tears in her eyes and felt sure he was not unmoved by her distress. "I thought Petra had a sort of beauty, now I think there is savagery as well."

"I think in a way, *kyria,* that you allude to me." He sat down at the table and cut himself a hunk of bread; pieces of the seeded crust flaked off and he popped them into his mouth. "Do you refuse to believe that I can have my moments of tractability?"

"I think there are times when you play the dove in hawk's feathers." She poured the coffee and kept her eyes demurely lowered as she spoke. "I think you use a certain natural power to charm for your own ends."

"Meaning I have no natural tenderness?"

"It makes you impatient not to have your own way. You like people to give in to you, and I shiver to think what you're like when you really lose your temper."

"Are you planning to find out?" He ate bacon and egg, and quirked an appreciative eyebrow. "You spoke about

117

finding another inn, but you know there is ample room for you at the villa."

"As companion to Ariadne." Hebe sprinkled vinegar on her bacon.

"But you find her appealing, so the objection can only be that I am her father and you would be subject to my orders."

"Yes . . ." Hebe dared his eyes and saw a slumbering threat in them, a look of lazy pursuit, letting her know he was the hunter and she the quarry. "I – I'll take care of Dee, but I won't accept a salary!"

"But don't be absurd." His look flashed to meet hers. "You can't work for me and not be paid."

"To be paid would spoil it, somehow." She gave him a look that she hoped was more brave than her heart in that moment. "I'm not being mutinous, it's just that I want to feel free; to be Dee's friend rather than her monitor."

"To accept payment from me would make you feel you were in some sort of bondage, eh?"

"Something of the sort. My board and bed will be payment enough. For the rest just let me enjoy my holiday with Ariadne."

"You say it as if you are afraid I would insist on a contract and keep you here beyond the limit of your endurance." He spoke with a thin and rather savage smile. "Unpaid you are free to go whenever you choose, eh? Well, if that is the way you want it, Miss Lawnay, then I shall not argue over the matter. I am happy to acquire your services at such a low cost, three or four meals a day and a bed at night."

"Don't forget," now she could smile because, albeit sardonically, he had given in to her request, "that I shall be saving money. I should have to pay for eating and

118

sleeping at an inn. Is the Firefly Taverna damaged beyond repair for Lefkes and his wife? I do hope not! It is their living."

"No, it can be put to rights, but naturally this will take a few weeks and they can't take guests. It was fortunate that only yourself and Mrs. Hilton were booked in at the present time. Petra is not on the tourist route, but the occasional visitor arrives."

"Both Mrs. Hilton and myself had a reason for coming –" And there Hebe broke off as Ariadne came running into the kitchen, great tears in her eyes and a sob in her throat. "It's a little goat and he's been hurt – you must c-come and see. You must!" She rushed at Hebe in her distress, as if her father weren't there. "His leg is all twisted and he's c-crying!"

"Hush now," Hebe took hold of her and held her. "Of course we'll come and look, Dee. Now don't upset yourself like this . . . where did you see the little goat?"

"Down by the temple." The tears rolled freely down the young face which only a short while ago had been so eager and impish. "The stone man fell on him –"

"What do you say, child?" Nikos Stephanos came striding round the table and his hands took firm hold of his small daughter. "Come, tell me what has happened. What is this about the stone man?"

But she struggled against his touch, pulling to get away from him, back into Hebe's arms.

"*Your* statue," she flung at him. "It's all broken and s-some of it fell on the little goat –"

Hebe gave him a swift look and saw the tightening of his jaw, the movement of that small muscle near his mouth, the only indication, sometimes, that he was moved or upset. The rest of his face was bronze and hard, the black brows slashing a line above the unreadable eyes.

"We must go and look," she said to him, and in this strange moment they were linked by the trembling body of Ariadne, and it was almost as if they were fighting for possession of her. Abruptly he released the child and swung on his heel. He left the kitchen and Hebe knew that he was going to the temple . . . she caught at Ariadne's hand and they followed passing Zea, with sheets in her arms, who wanted to know why the *kyrios* had a face like thunder.

"A small animal has been hurt," Hebe hastily explained. "It seems the statue fell in the little garden temple –"

"The stone god?" The sheets fell in a bundle from Zea's arms as she crossed herself. "It's a bad omen, *kyria*. If the statue is broken –"

"It is, all broken." Ariadne was pulling impatiently at Hebe's hand. "We must go and get the little goat! *He'll kill it!*"

"Don't be silly, Dee!" Hebe spoke with a chiding note in her voice, but all the same she quickened her pace and they were both running when they came in sight of the temple. A gasp of horror escaped her . . . the dome was cracked sheer across and the front of the little building sagged on broken columns. Down the steps lay strewn the torso and head of the stone Adonais. The earthquake had done it, yet it looked at first glance like the work of a vandal . . . as if someone had come along with an axe and chopped the statue down.

The man it had so strangely resembled knelt on the ground beside a small shape that lay unnaturally still. With a sharp little scream Ariadne buried her face against Hebe. "I hate him – I hate him –" she sobbed. "He's cruel and wicked –"

He glanced slowly up at Hebe and his expression was stony. "There was no other way," he said, without emotion. "The animal was hurt internally – if it had been only the leg it could have been helped."

"You knew we were on our way," Hebe hated him. with her eyes and her voice. "You could have removed the animal before you – you didn't have to let Dee see you."

"The creature was in agony." He stood up, the little dead goat in his arms, the pathetic head lolling against his shirtfront. "It must be buried ... did you not ask me, *kyria*, if sacrifices are still made to the pagan gods on this island? They are, but not always with intention."

He went off among the trees, and a sudden wind stirred the long eucalyptus leaves and the aroma was like an incense, clouding about Hebe and intensifying the paganism of the place and the moment.

She stared at the broken stone figure on the temple steps, and she held Ariadne tightly to her. "Come away, darling," she murmured. "It had to be done, and I'm sure your father did it as painlessly as possible."

"He's wicked," Ariadne insisted, in a choked voice. "Nanna said he was, for taking me away from her. She said it would be a curse on him a-and I wish the statue had fallen on him!"

"Dee – please – you mustn't say such things." Hebe drew her away from the blasted temple and took her home. "I'd love to see your doll's house. I had one as a child, but I bet your one is nicer. I hear it has real furniture carved by your Uncle Stavros."

Dee stood blinking her long, wet lashes, then she nodded and they climbed the spiral staircase to the attic which was her own special playroom, stretching from one oriel window to another, the walls painted with flowers and fun figures, and filled with the toys of a lonely child who had no playmates.

There was a dappled rocking horse with a scarlet saddle, a large family of dolls, and several large woolly animals. There were shelves of books, puzzle games and paint-boxes. And predominantly there was the doll's house, a treasure trove of the most delightful miniature furniture Hebe had ever seen. She and Ariadne spent the rest of the morning dusting it all and re-arranging the rooms, which were papered and carpeted and hung with tiny lamps on chains, just like those in the *saloni*.

Hebe had been torn with doubts about staying at the villa, but as the morning passed in the company of Ariadne, and she saw the stricken look fade from the doe-brown eyes, she became more certain that she had a sort of duty to remain. It was almost as if the child's sanity depended on her, for still there rang in her mind those un-childlike phrases . . . words like hate . . . the wish that her father be cursed.

Quite casually Hebe said to her: "I'm going to stay for a few weeks and be with you each day. Will you like that?"

The big eyes, slanting like a doe's, dwelt with a sort of hunger on Hebe's face. "You are going to be my *nou-nou*?"

"Yes, Dee. I'm going to be your *nounou*."

CHAPTER VIII

HAVING by the afternoon put his own house in fair working order, Nikos Stephanos announced that he was going to the mainland in the *caique* to collect building materials and bedding for those in the village who had lost their homes. He told Zea, who passed on the information to Hebe. While Ariadne took her nap, Hebe was reading a book in the pillared loggia at the side of the house, overlooking the dense and fragrant lemon groves.

She took the glass of lemon tea which Zea had brought her, and she looked surprised by the news. "Does he actually have some feeling for those poor people, Zea? He seems to me so proud and adamant."

"He has a business to run, *kyria*, and some of his workmen lost their homes."

"I see —"

"Perhaps not quite, *kyria*. It would be hard for a Greek not to feel sorry for the women who have lost their household treasures, those things from the dowry, the hand-carved furniture and the hand-sewn linen. The flower vases for the icons, and the framed pictures of children who have gone to another country. The household is precious to a Greek person; the family is most important. For us death is very final, so we cling to the things which still bear the likeness or the touch of a relative."

Hebe sipped her deliciously cool tea, and the thought struck her like a tiny arrow that in coming to stay at the villa she was bound to learn disquieting things about the master of the house. It was a kind of protection to believe him arrogant and ruthless . . . but he was other things as well. He was the man whom Daphne had known in Boston. He was the boy whom Zea had known during the years she had worked for his mother.

"You know him better than I." She smiled with a dash of bravado. "I suppose when he was younger he was easier to . . . like?"

"He was, perhaps, too easy to love." And with this enigmatic remark Zea departed, leaving Hebe alone in the shade and stillness of the loggia, while the hot Greek sun distilled a heady fragrance from the lemon trees.

With some difficulty, because the hard and forceful, fully adult male kept intruding, she envisaged a much younger man, of such charm and attraction that no girl could resist him. In fact a girl like Cicely, indulged by her parents and used to having her own way, might have set out to dazzle the young Greek with her blonde hair and her blue eyes. She might have gone to his head like a rare young wine, and for her sake he had settled in America and for a few years he had lived the kind of life which she enjoyed. One of gaiety and theatres; country clubs and dinner parties . . . until, with the sudden Doric longing for the simple things, the silvery rocks, the scent of herbs and the smell of fleece, the taste of the wild growing fig, he had returned to Greece and being so unalterably Greek had insisted that his wife come with him.

Perhaps he had left Ariadne in the care of Cicely's mother because he doubted that his wife would settle down in Greece . . . perhaps there had been quarrels he had not wanted the child to overhear . . . Hebe could almost see it all in startling detail, he with all his Greek dominance asking of his American wife, who loved city life and the wearing of lovely clothes, to love in their place the island of stone.

Then all at once she had fallen from the Rock of Helios and died . . . and if Zea had ever heard them quarrelling she had, from Greek loyalty, kept the knowledge to herself. She would know from her own full knowledge of life that the boundary line between love and hate was a finely woven thread and that it could be snapped in a moment of fury. No one would never know the real truth, unless he chose to tell it, and Hebe felt certain that his lips could lock like iron and hold prisoner what he chose not to reveal.

At dinner that evening she could have asked Daphne what she thought of the change in Nikos since last they had met, but Hebe decided to be cautious. Daphne might leap to the conclusion that she was attracted by him . . . in reality Hebe was haunted by the thought of Cicely. She seemed to linger, frail and fair, in the arched corridors of the villa, restless and seeking. A shadow unseen and yet there, like a vagrant hint of perfume.

"Is there a piano in the place?" Daphne demanded of Zea when she brought coffee to them.

"Yes, *kyria,* but it isn't used since . . . since the wife of the *kyrios* died."

"Why not, for heaven's sake? This house needs livening up and I thought Cicely would have a piano. She played quite well, I remember, having been taught at a smart finishing school for young ladies on Long Island. I learned from a fellow I used to know – I don't read music, but I have a good ear for a lively tune." Daphne flashed her most persuasive smile at Zea. "In which room in this Doric mansion does the *kyrios* keep the piano? I mean, it's almost a year since Cicely died and no man can mourn for ever, not even an intense Greek."

"There is a music room." Zea made irritated noises with the big bunch of keys that she carried in a pocket of her black dress; like many another Greek woman she had worn black ever since her husband had died, and that had been while Alik was still a baby. "I shall have to unlock the room and it may be rather cold."

"Then we will need a fire to keep us warm," said Daphne with a queenly air. "Strange how cool it becomes when that burning sun goes down. I suppose it's the contrast."

"Sometimes our nights are warm and then the nightingales sing." Zea spoke with a beady-eyed glance at Daphne, and Hebe wondered how long it would be before these two flared into active argument. Zea was used to being in charge here when the master was absent, and Daphne had obviously decided that from now on *she* was going to give orders and enliven the house.

Hebe checked a smile . . . she liked Zea and had an idea that Daphne had met her match. "There is no wood prepared for fires yet, madam. You will have to wear your fur coat if you feel cold."

"Really!" Daphne arched her eyebrows. "Where is you son? Can't he go and collect some wood? All that hubble-bubble last night must have knocked down a few trees, and I notice there's a forest almost on the back steps."

"Those are lemon trees, madam, and my son has gone to the mainland with the *kyrios*. The *caique* will not return until tomorrow."

"Mmm, well I don't fancy shivering, so we had better stay here in the *saloni*. I notice this room has a fixed electric fire."

126

"It is here that the *kyrios* spends many of his evening hours." Zea said it with great dignity.

"What, all alone?" Daphne glanced around her. "It has an oriental air ... a touch of Turkish splendour. Mmm, I rather like it. Perhaps the piano could be moved in here?"

Zea's eyes flashed with Greek fire. "I would not suggest such a thing if I were you, madam!"

"Why ever not?" Daphne arranged herself on the divan, spreading out the full skirt of her brocade dress. "He could then lounge like a sultan while I played to him. I'm quite sure he would enjoy it ... and I'm not being hard-hearted. A man can't mourn till doomsday, even if it is part of the Greek tradition. Besides, it isn't good for the chickadee. She really is a pretty thing – okay, Zea, that will be all."

Hebe didn't dare to look at Zea as with a rustle of starched black skirts she withdrew from the *saloni*. Daphne was being impossibly high-handed, and she had only been in the house a day!

"You are giving me a disapproving look, sweetie." Daphne gave her full-throated laugh. "Come and have your coffee and don't worry your head over that officious housekeeper. It seems to me that it's about time a woman gave a few orders around here – you take cream and sugar, of course? With your fine-boned frame you don't need to keep off sweet things, or do high-strung nerves keep you slim? Do relax, or are you a cat that prowls?"

Hebe smiled, aware of the swing of her tawny hair as she sat down on a floor cushion, circular and plump, and took her coffee with a murmur of thanks. "I don't think you ought to antagonize Zea. She's been awfully good to Mr. Stephanos and the little girl. She left her own island,

127

Andelos, to come here, and it's a far more comfortable place. Fewer earthquakes and not so many ruins."

"I thought we'd all be buried alive." Daphne shuddered. "When Nikos turned up this morning it was like seeing the Angel Gabriel. What a stroke of fate, Hebe, that we should both be landed on him. Isn't he fabulous? Tragedy suits him, he's even better-looking than he was in Boston. Terribly Greek and grave, with those deep, dense eyes, and his mouth all controlled against a woman. What do you think of him?"

The question was not unexpected, yet it left Hebe at a loss for a reply. What could she say about a man who might, in a moment of fury, have killed his wife? All she knew for sure was that she stayed here because a child had clung to her hand.

"He throws you, eh?" Daphne drawled. "It's the first time you've met a man with a streak of ruthlessness. You're young and sort of innocent, so perhaps you don't know that women are just a bit fascinated by the men who make them feel afraid."

"I'm not fascinated," Hebe protested. "He isn't at all the kind of person I like. I'd leave this house tomorrow if I didn't feel that Ariadne needs me. She was upset this morning . . . she found a young goat that had been hurt by falling masonry . . . her father had to put it out of its misery. She takes things to heart."

"Then watch out, Hebe, because I believe you do as well." Daphne ran her painted gaze over the unpainted face of the English girl. "In lots of ways you are desperately innocent, but I grew up in a tough part of New York and if I ever had any girlish dreams they are long forgotten. I only know that if you want something badly enough, you grab for it, and if it stings you then you don't

128

cry. The marriage I grabbed at gave me luxury but it didn't give me love . . . the next time I want love."

"From Nikos Stephanos?" Hebe had spoken the words before she could stop them, then all too clearly her skin showed a vivid blush. "I'm sorry . . . it's none of my business."

"No, sweetie." Daphne snapped open a little jewelled bag and took from it a thin cigarette case and a lighter initialled with a jewel. "I am the guest here and you are the governess and we won't confuse our respective positions, will we? I understand you have a small room close to the child's?"

"Yes, it overlooks the lemon groves," Hebe said quietly.

"Really? My room is quite splendid and at the front of the house . . all that dark carved furniture is fine in its way, but if I had my way I'd change it all for whitewood and golden pine, and pastel-tint the walls of the rooms. The Villa Helios could be made into a gem, positioned as it is above the sea, with all that sparkling light during the day. Those crowding lemon trees could be cut back –"

"But they've such a wonderful scent!" Hebe looked shocked by this suggested vandalism; it actually hurt her feelings to think of those delicate, dark-foliaged trees being cut down. She looked at Daphne with incredulous eyes, and saw a woman to whom nothing really mattered except the achieving of her own goals. She was totally self-absorbed, living only for her own matt skin, her own glossy hair, her own inclinations, whether they be sensual or cruel.

"I prefer Chanel, whatever the number, my sweet." Daphne smiled through her cigarette smoke. "You're quite the little nature girl, aren't you? Be careful not to be too elusive or you will be the untouched spinster. What a fate for a woman!"

"I imagine there are lots of women who never marry because they lost the man they loved. Natural tragedies can change the course of one's life, and there are compensations."

"What, caring for another woman's child?"

"Perhaps." Hebe glanced down at her interlocked hands, and realised that they were trembling slightly. She was honest, and courageous in her own way, but she was no match for the ruthless wit of a woman like Daphne. "For a while, anyway. I'm only the stop-gap until Dee's proper governess arrives, then I return to London to take up a career."

"I hope it won't be a panacea." With a touch of smiling malice Daphne rose and went to the drinks cabinet. She had a sway to her walk, a debonair quality, like that of a well-trained actress. "They say to love the child is to love the man . . . ah, I see he hasn't quite succumbed to uncivilized habits. Do you like Napoleon brandy?"

"I don't want anything to drink, thank you." Hebe had to make an effort to speak politely, for it had now become evident that Daphne was baiting her; that her aura of friendship had given way to the hostility of a woman who was enduring no rivals for the friendship or the affection of Nikos Stephanos. By some stroke of fate, nefarious or otherwise, he was now free, and Daphne wanted him. She desired all that hard, proud masculinity and she didn't care that he had no tenderness to give.

"Well, I'm going to treat myself to the comforts of the house." Daphne returned to the divan with a generous portion of the tawny brandy in one of the carved bowls Hebe remembered from the night before. Not the devil's nightcap, after all, but the favourite wine of a dictator who had loved beautiful women.

"So how long does this temporary job last?" The question was casual as a thread of silk.

"It isn't a job." Hebe felt a little stab of satisfaction in being able to reveal this. "I'm doing it as a favour and I shan't be paid."

"A favour?" Daphne stared at her. "You are full of surprises. You mean you are going to be a sort of holiday auntie, all done out of the goodness of your heart? Are you sure Nikos hasn't touched your heart?"

"If such a man ever touched my heart, I'd leave Petra to get away from him." Hebe rose to her feet, feeling a need to get away from Daphne's innuendoes and her sultry perfume. She had not known that Nikos Stephanos would be away from home this evening; she had dressed herself in a sumptuous dress and it had been wasted on Hebe. She was annoyed and Hebe wasn't staying to be used as an outlet.

"I think I'll take a stroll before going to bed." Hebe walked to the door. "The starlight is bright and clear to-night –"

"Restless, honey? Like the little cat you remind me of, with those green eyes and that cat-gold hair?"

"At least I don't scratch." Hebe withdrew from the room and closed the door with a sense of relief. She had quite liked Daphne at the taverna, but now they were both installed at the villa the other woman's manner had undergone a change. It was as if the atmosphere brought out something primitive in her, and with a little shiver Hebe crossed the hall to fetch her coat from her room. The heels of her shoes pattered intrusively on the Greek tiling, patterned black and white in that ancient key design.

Shadow lay pooled beneath the low, wide arches, and the jasmine that glimmered in a big stone pot seemed to tremble slightly like the skirt of a woman's dress.

Suddenly Hebe was running up the stairs as if something were at her heels, and she knew when she reached her room that she couldn't go down into that shadowy hall again tonight. She flooded her bedroom with light and breathed a sigh of relief when she saw her familiar toiletries on the dressing-table, and her nightwear and robe across the stool at the foot of the bed.

Throwing her coat about her shoulders like a cloak, she went out on her flower-hung veranda and breathed deeply the night scent of the lemon trees. How far she felt from her home town, from the sound of the church bells tolling the hour, sweet and musical and unlike the bold, commanding sound of Greek bells.

Here at night the stars seemed to burn in the sky, shedding a radiance over the garden below, haunted by great white moths and the throbbing of cicadas. She thought of the little temple and the shattered statue . . . and all those dolls that stared with glass eyes in the attic where Ariadne played alone. It was immaterial what Daphne Hilton thought and said . . . for these few weeks on the isle of Petra she would try to make happy the little girl whose skin was softly brown, like a Botticelli rose, and whose eyes held the bewilderment and the rebellion of the lonely child.

"Nounou . . . Nounou!" Ariadne ran in to wake her when morning came. She climbed on to the bed and wormed her way beneath the covers. She lay there smiling into Hebe's face. "Can we go to the beach today . . . can we go in the water . . . and can we take our lunch and not come home for hours and hours?"

"Would you like to do all that, Dee?"

"Please!" A young cheek rested against Hebe's, and she was shot through by a tiny arrow of pain . . . it had happened again, her heart had opened to this child and the wrench would be all the harder to bear when the time came to part from her.

The sun smiled on them and they swam and paddled about in the warm shallows, and ate their picnic lunch in the shade of a clump of pink tamarisks. It grew too hot to play, so Hebe read a story to Ariadne until the young head drooped and she curled up to sleep on the tawny pelt of the sand, with a cushion beneath her head. Hebe watched the sea as it came running to the shore, all sparkle and foam as it struck the rocks.

Up at the villa Daphne would be taking her siesta and planning what she would wear to greet Nikos when he returned home. Tonight he would dine with them and sit with them in the *saloni*, and Hebe could feel her nerves and her body tensing against those evening hours to come. She knew in advance that Daphne meant to play the siren to his pagan Greek, and if there had not been tragic elements to the villa, shadowing its beauty like a veil over a sad face, Hebe might have found amusing the prospect of a duel of words between a worldly woman and a man who could drive home a point with relentless precision . . . just as he might drive in a nail when planking one of his strong and graceful *caiques*.

Ariadne slept soundly, but Hebe was restless and she rose to her feet and trod the sand to the water's edge, where the sea-urchins clung tenaciously to the streaming rocks. The pattern of life on Petra seemed to be one of struggle, and Hebe could not imagine Daphne liking it here for very long. Like Cicely her desire for the man would clash with her love of worldly things ... Like Cicely ...

Hebe didn't dare to look beyond that thought, and she plunged into the waves and struck out through the glistening, heaving water. It tossed her and played with her like a live thing, and this was what she wanted. When evening came she wanted to be lazily immune from the tensions and the remarks. She wished her part in the drama to be a very minor one.

She described a curve in the water and headed for the beach ... she was hauling herself to the sands when she glanced all the way up the fire-coloured cliffs and saw someone standing there, very still, as if part of the sky and the sun. Her pulse-beat knew him, though her eyes were too dazzled by the sunshine to be able to make out his face. His height and his stance were enough, and then he drew back out of sight and she plunged wet and startled through the sand to where her bath towel lay crumpled. She wiped herself down and wrung the water from her hair.

So he was back from his errand of mercy, and she knelt there, almost as if asking the gods that they keep him from coming down to the cove. Then a stone rattled and fell and she knew, with a tensing of her body, that he was making his way down the path to the shore.

The air was heavy with the scent of the sea and the stone-pines. The sun-crazed cicadas purred away like mad, and when a long shadow fell over Hebe she had to brace herself to look upwards. Her sea-tousled hair fell across her cheek, and her eyes were green and turbulent as the sea.

"You look like Andromeda unchained from her rock,"

he said, and his gaze played over her with the rapidity of a flame, before leaping to the child who lay curled on the sand with a spotted, long-eared dog of wool clasped in her arms.

Hebe reached quickly for her towelling jacket that zipped at the front, letting the damp swing of her hair hide from him the sting of colour in her cheeks as she covered herself, all but her long lightly tanned legs. He looked as if he had come straight from the *caique*, darkly burned by the salty air, with the sailing light still intense in his eyes. His shirt was bunched above the belt of his trousers, and his sleeves were rolled above the vigour of his forearms. He looked every inch the Greek sailor, with a lethal grace of body and authority stamped upon his face instead of a carefree smile.

"You have had a good day?" he asked.

"A very happy one." Her arms tightened about her up-drawn knees as he sprawled out on the sands, holding his right arm in an odd, almost cradling position across his chest where his shirt was bunched. "As you can see, Ariadne has tired herself out with her exertions. She's a sturdy little swimmer, *kyrios*."

"Excellent." His teeth gleamed a moment, white against the dark skin of his face. "A Greek likes to hear that his offspring is sound of limb and courageous. That is how I want Ariadne to grow up, unafraid of the world ... a little tigress rather than a lamb."

Hebe smiled slightly, and then she realized that at the back of his words lay more than arrogance. Ariadne was his daughter, and as she grew up she was going to have to live with the things that were said about him ... and oh, to look at him was to see a man who might know all the rites of paganism. The black slant of his brows, the well-deep darkness of his eyes, the mocking quirk at the side of his mouth . . . these were not the attributes of a tame and conventional man.

Hebe glanced at his child, and saw the trace of mutiny about the small chin . . . yes, she would need to be like him to combat the world, which would try and hurt Nikos Stephanos' lovely daughter.

A wild desire to demand the real, or the innocent truth, shot through Hebe, but the words died on her lips when she saw him take from his shirtfront a small puppy dog with drooping ears and an absurd stump of a tail.

"I found him abandoned among the ruins of a house, a scrap of woe which might take the child's persistent young mind off that young goat." His gaze lifted from the puppy to Hebe's face, which expressed delight and surprise. "What do you think? I never dared to give her a pet before in case she smothered it with love."

"She'll be thrilled." Even as his words struck Hebe as a trifle strange, she held out her arms for the puppy. "May I hold him? Has he been fed? Ah, he is a pretty little scrap!"

"You may hold him, and we fed him with some goat milk Zea had ready for her cheese making."

The puppy snuggled up against Hebe, while Nikos straightened his shirt and tucked it into his belt. His action in bringing home the orphaned puppy made him seem terribly human . . . Hebe in that moment almost liked him.

"Was your trip to the mainland a satisfactory one?" she asked. "Zea told me why you went. She said some of your workmen had suffered the loss of their homes."

"Yes. Stavros and I are shutting down the boatyard while the men build new homes. The villagers will help them, and then there will be a celebration . . . dancing and food, a sort of propitiation of the gods." His eyes dwelt on Hebe, brilliantly dark and yet fathomless. "Does it all seem very pagan to you?"

"Not really. My uncle once told me that when the war ended in England the people filled the streets with bunting and set up feast tables in front of the ruins and made merry because their troubles were over and they could build again the homes they had lost." She lowered her gaze and stroked the puppy. "Perhaps deep in all our bones there is a touch of the pagan."

"For the British, after all, were still barbaric while the Greeks were laying water pipes and writing plays," he drawled.

"We and our land were green, but we learned quickly. You must admit, *kyrios*, that if Greece was the cradle of civilization, we were the mother of common sense. We realized that if men spent much of their time idolising stone gods, the corn went to seed in the fields and the fish swam away before the nets could catch them."

"Yes, the British have always enjoyed the material things. They bake a good pie, weave a fine wool and erect firm walls, but the divinity of the body, as expressed by Greek art, they shrink from, or shrug off as unimportant. Why, I wonder, are you people so coy of beauty when often a British face has more loveliness than a flower? I told you of my cousin who has an English wife . . . she is, perhaps, the most beautiful creature I have ever seen, but when she first married Paul she was cooler than any statue in a Greek garden. She had to live in Greece in order to come fully alive; to discover love as a pagan delight rather than a matter of submission. Love is not a possession to be worn like a pendant, which a woman shows off to other people and then puts away in a box for the night . . . ah,

137

but you don't want to hear of that."

"I'm curious even if I am not personally interested." Hebe, in fact, was a little shocked by the extent of her curiosity . . . was he referring to Cicely when he spoke of being shown off to other people? Had she been a woman who loved with her eyes rather than her emotions? Had she wanted him to be of stone rather than flesh and blood?

"It is just as well that you have no personal inclination to love a Greek." He sprang to his feet and seemed to tower above her in a rather frightening way. "The hawk and the dove are not meant for mating."

He said it so harshly that his voice awoke Ariadne. She sat up with a start, her fawn-coloured hair, fine as wild silk, tumbling about her bewildered face. "Nounou . . .?"

"Look, darling, what your father brought you to play with." Hebe showed her the puppy, and even as delight filled the child's eyes, her father was striding away towards the path that was roughly hewn in the cliffs. "The sun will be going down in a short while," he called back over his shoulder. "Don't play too long, *poulakis*."

He leapt up the path and was soon out of sight . . . little birds, he had called them. Fledglings, with time to play together before the sun grew cool and the shadows fell.

"Nounou, what shall we call him?" Ariadne was cuddling the little dog so close to her that she was in danger of smothering him. He yelped and struggled, and Hebe explained, with a gentle firmness, that he was only a baby dog and mustn't be held so tightly or he would be hurt. He wasn't like Jason, the woolly dog. He would have to be fed and groomed and at night he would sleep in a basket and not in Ariadne's bed.

"But why not?" Ariadne fondled his ears. "He'll be much warmer and he won't be afraid if he's with Jason and me. It's lonely being in bed all by yourself."

"Well, you might roll on him and smother him."

"Like the little goat?" Ariadne cast a look of horror at Hebe. "I don't want the puppy to die. I love him . . . he's all warm and furry and he wriggles. Nounou, I want him to be mine for always."

"He is yours, Dee. Your father gave him to you. Now what about a name for him?"

The child considered this, giving it all her attention, her young brows slanting wing-like above her eyes, so that her likeness to Nikos was amazingly apparent. Hebe studied her and wondered if Cicely had resented the ecstasy and the pain of becoming a mother. Was it possible to deduce from his cynical remark that his wife had desired only to be gay and decorative; the envy of other women because she had a good-looking Greek for a husband?

Hebe felt a stab of pain and realized that she had bitten her lip. She could almost see him . . . almost hear the anger in his voice . . . he was no actor to be stared at. He was a Greek and it was time for Cicely to have his Greek child!

"Hercules!"

"What?" Hebe gave Ariadne a startled look.

"That's what I'm going to call my puppy. Do you like it?"

"It's a big name for a little dog."

"Then I'll shorten it to Curly until he grows up – but I don't want him to grow up too quickly."

"No, darling. It's nice to stay young and carefree."

The sun was firing the sky when they climbed slowly the path that led to the villa. When they reached the headland Ariadne ran on ahead to see Alik about a basket for Curly. Hebe stood and lingered a few moments, as if

139

gathering her resources for the evening to come. Above her in the sky a hawk circled another, wide-winged, dark against the golden fire spreading from the sun. Below the sea was reddening as the sun sank towards it ... soon night's black shadows would fall over the island and then the stars would radiate.

There was rarely a moment when a sort of beauty did not soften the wildness and stony grandeur of Petra. It had a soul, and Hebe was very aware of this as she stood on the spot Nikos Stephanos had chosen to gaze down at the beach. He had watched her emerge from the sea, and she wondered if it was then he had been reminded of Cicely.

She like Hebe had been fair of skin and hair, and then as the wind agitated the tousled hair at the nape of Hebe's neck, she turned away from the awesome sun setting low over the sea and hurried towards the gate that led into the garden of the villa.

To her dismay it was locked, and she guessed that Demitriades had seen Ariadne and assumed that Hebe was home as well. She called his name through the iron-work of the gate, but he didn't appear to let her in, clad in his black leggings and breeches and boldly embroidered shirt.

Well, she couldn't stay here ... soon it would be quite dark, and already a chilly wind was blowing from the sea and creeping about her legs. She studied the gate and wondered if she could climb over it. Why not? Its lacing of iron would make firm footholds and she had often shinned up trees in the wake of Dion. She tossed the picnic things over the gate, and then with resolution she began to haul herself up the gate towards the iron palings along the top of it. That proved the tricky part, hoisting herself

140

over those spear-like points and clinging with all her might to the lacing of iron below them in order to find a foothold for the climb down.

She made it after a strenuous ten minutes or so, and feeling breathlessly adventurous she was about to step off the gate when a firm pair of arms swung her to the ground. "Are you out of your mind?" a voice demanded.

She knew the strength of those arms and all she wanted was to be out of them. "The gate was locked – it was climb over or fast for my supper until Demitriades made his rounds. Y-you can let go of me – I'm all right."

Instead he swung her to face him and in the fading light his features were stern. "I was about to have a smoke before dinner when I heard some calls echoing through the garden. I thought it was a bird and didn't pay much attention, but I might have guessed it was the English Miss who had got into some bother. You could easily have fallen, you realize!"

"But I didn't." She gave a laugh, and he shook her. "Really! What was I to do? You said you heard me calling, but you didn't hurry to find out if anything was wrong. I was getting cold, standing locked out like a cat for the night."

His hands tightened, feeling her lack of clothing through the jacket that barely reached to her knees. "What kept you? Ariadne was in the kitchen with the boy when I came out for my smoke."

"I was watching the sunset. It was rather glorious," she added, with a touch of shyness. "At home in England I live near the sea, but our sunsets are far more timid."

"Unlike English girls," he drawled. "I wonder what it would take to really unnerve you?" Then as if driven to find out, he pulled her close to him and his left hand grip-

141

ped her hair and drew back her head so her face and her neck were exposed to him. She was too dismayed to move, feeling his grip on her hair and aware that if she tried to pull away it would hurt like the devil. The pallor of her face gleamed against his darkness, and his eyes burned with an oddly reckless blaze as they held hers. For moments that seemed to last endlessly she suffered him to hold her, then as panic took possession of her she fought with him, whip-supple, and gave a cry as her hair was tugged by his fingers.

Perhaps she let loose the devil that might have been stilled by her stillness, for the cry she gave was snatched away and her entire being felt the flame and the fury of his down-driving kiss. His mouth bruised her and his arms felt as if they'd break her ... then he thrust her away from him and she stumbled over the picnic things, saving herself against the trunk of a tree. The scent of the eucalyptus was so pungent that it brought tears to her eyes. "You have no sense of right or wrong," she accused. "Y-you aren't going to drag me down to your level of decadence ... I'm leaving here tonight!"

"You can't," he said, "unless you want to hurt Ariadne far more than I could have hurt you. What is a kiss, *kyria*? Surely you have been kissed by the young man whose name I heard on your lips."

"Dion was everything you could never be. He was never a satyr!"

"Was he too much a saint to treat you like a woman? That is all I have done." Nikos Stephanos gave a mocking laugh. "One would think I had dishonoured you."

"To be kissed by you is the nearest thing I know to being degraded."

"Thank you for the compliment." He picked up the

picnic things and walked ahead of her through the dark garden. He knew every inch of the way as if by instinct, and when they reached the house he bowed her in through the door. Mockery was moulded to his face like a mask.

"Miss Lawnay?"

"Yes?" She gave him a look that defied him to apologise for his atrocious behaviour.

"I warn you not to break your promise to Ariadne."

"I'm fond of her, but I signed no contract to stay under your roof."

"I thought your word good enough." The mockery vanished and his features took on a merciless look. "I may not be your dream of an immortal lover, *kyria*, but I can promise you that I make a very mortal enemy. Break that child's heart and I will be to you both the things I mention."

She stood there, not a tinge of colour in her face as she looked at him, warned by every nerve in her body that he would keep his word ... if she left tonight and left Ariadne in tears, this man would ensure that she cried even bitterer tears. The threat of it burned in his eyes ... Ariadne was the only creature he loved, and Hebe knew with a turning over of her heart that she could not defy him. He made her afraid for herself, but it was his love of Dee that made her say, huskily:

"Very well. I'll stay for your daughter's sake, but don't ever touch me again. Keep your cruel hands off me!"

She turned from him and left these words in the air behind her ... when she reached her room, she felt a sudden weakness in her legs and was glad to flop across her bed.

A nervous tremor shook her from head to toe ... he had not spared her, and she had not spared him ... and after such a scene she could not sit at the dining table with him.

She put on a blouse and skirt and went down to the kitchen. She sat in the alcove with Ariadne and they ate a meal together. Afterwards they went to the attic to play a while with Curly. Then he was made comfortable in the old wicker bread basket Alik had found for him, and Hebe bathed Ariadne and put her to bed.

When she bent to kiss the child on the cheek, the young arms curled around her and hugged her. "You are the best *nounou* I ever had," she whispered. "I don't mind not being with Nanna now you're here, and I wish you could stay for ever."

"I can only stay until your regular governess arrives, Dee. Then I must go and start work in London."

"But that won't be for a long time yet." Ariadne smiled happily. "Good night, Nounou."

"Good night, my pet."

Hebe lowered the little night lamp to a glimmer, for the child didn't like sleeping in the dark, then she withdrew from the room and quietly closed the door behind her. She walked on quiet feet along the gallery, and then suddenly she came to a halt and stood in the shadow of one of the columns that arcaded the gallery. Down below in the hall she had caught the sound of laughter ... Daphne and Nikos were on their way to the *saloni*. Their figures passed within the range of her vision. Daphne was dressed like a priestess of ancient rites in deep red silk, and her dark hair was clasped in a shimmering diamond bird with spread wings. She looked dramatic, and she sounded pleased to have Nikos to herself.

Perhaps she sensed that he and Hebe had quarrelled. She tilted her face to him as he opened the door of the *saloni.* "I do love this room, Nikos." Her words echoed across the silent hall. "It makes me feel like the favourite of the *harem.*"

He laughed, and that too echoed across the hall. They entered the room and the door closed. Hebe wandered to the end of the gallery and sat in the curved sill of the oriel window. Her hair was swept back from her brow and clipped in a bronze buckle. Her profile was pensive . . . she might have been Columbine sitting in the curve of the moon.

CHAPTER IX

It wasn't an easy thing to forget, that Nikos Stephanos had crushed her mouth with his and that upon his lips there had been a tang of Turkish cheroot and a flavour of lemon, as if he had been chewing a sprig as he walked through the garden.

He had been monstrous, and had taken pleasure in being so! Hebe kept out of his way in the days that followed, filled as they were with golden sunlight and places to explore. She was careful to take Ariadne in the opposite direction to the places he took Daphne, who was enjoying every exclusive moment of his company. How annoying it was to run into them the day Alik took Hebe and her charge, not forgetting Curly, to see the cavern of the virgins, in which the island girls were concealed when pirates had raided the island. Later on the big underground cave had been used to hide partisans and their supplies, during enemy occupation of the island.

"Fancy being herded in here!" Daphne exclaimed, looking out of place in her smart suit and bewitching straw hat. "I think I'd sooner have faced the pirates than all this grim dankness. What do you say, Hebe?"

"I'm sure Miss Lawnay has never found pirates to her liking," Nikos drawled. "She sees no glamour or thraldom in wickedness."

"The puritan type," Daphne smiled, patting Ariadne on the head and receiving a glare in return. "What a dear little ponytail girl you are, and so like your father to look at, especially when you frown."

Hebe shot a look at Nikos to see his reaction to this. His eyebrow quirked, but all he said was that he could hear the bells of the melon-seller's cart and Ariadne was to run and tell the man to cut six big slices.

"Six, Patir?" She did some counting. "There are only five of us."

"So there are, *mou*." His teeth gleamed in a smile. "Then you and Alik can share the extra slice between you."

"Smashing!" She ran off across the beach, where on this hot bright Sunday families lolled on the sands or explored the famous cavern.

"Smashing?" queried Nikos. "What a curious expression."

"It means," said Hebe, with dignity, "that your daughter is highly delighted."

"Really?" he said. "Surely it's more logical to be in a smashing mood when one is furious?"

"Delight is just as emotional – and it is inevitable that Dee will pick up certain expressions from me. I am sorry if you object."

"I was not chastising you, Miss Lawnay. I am merely intrigued that certain English words can have a double meaning." A sardonic smile flickered in his eyes, and Hebe felt a rise of colour to her cheeks. He wore a light linen suit and his hair was as groomed as a raven's wing . . . as Daphne slid a jewelled hand along his sleeve, Hebe turned away and went in the direction of the melon-seller's cart. Alik caught up with her and he said, gruffly:

"Do you think the *kyrios* is planning to marry the American woman?"

"I wouldn't know, Alik, but they seem well matched." Hebe's voice was cool as the ice in which the melon man

147

kept his green-gold wares on such a warm day. Ariadne was petting the donkey that pulled the small cart; his eyes and his coat were a velvety brown, and there were beads and bells attached to his harness.

"I wish I had a donkey," said Ariadne. "Do you think Patir will buy me one?"

Alik looked at her with brooding eyes, and then he bent his head and stroked the puppy. "I think the *kyrios* is going to give you a new mother," he muttered.

Ariadne stared at him, and then she rushed at Hebe and flung her arms around her, hugging her through the cool material of her sleeveless dress. "I want Patir to marry you and then you won't ever go away!"

It was said so loudly that heads turned, and Hebe was immediately aware of the crushing silence right behind her. Daphne and Nikos had approached in time to hear the child's remark, and Hebe wanted to sink into the sands of the beach, out of sight of everyone.

Marriage ... with him ... when it had taken only a kiss to spark off fury and threats and sleepless nights, when the stars burned beyond her window and she wished she had never seen the island of Petra.

On that crowded island beach there were people who knew him, people who had known Cicely. Their curious stares seemed to scorch Hebe, for the sun lit her hair to a pale gold, and she could feel their thoughts like a barrage of tiny and very painful arrows. Cicely had been fair and alien to their ways ... they were wondering if once again the dark *kyrios* was attracted to a foreign girl! Hebe could have told them the real truth of the matter, and it was frustrating that she must remain silent.

She dared not even look at him to see his reaction to his daughter's words; any glance at this precise and awkward

148

moment would have looked conspiratorial. So, with downcast eyes, Hebe ate her slice of melon and never afterwards could she recall its flavour or coolness. She burned from head to toe as if in a fever . . . and, indeed, she was in a fever of impatience to escape with Dee and Alik.

She was on the point of suggesting that they make for home, when Ariadne said in her bell-like voice: "Can I have a donkey as well?"

"Young lady," her father tilted her pointed chin with a forefinger, "you are going to have to learn that you can't have everything you set your eyes on. The world isn't a great big candy jar, you know. One doesn't buy donkeys – or wives – at the request of a half-pint daughter."

"A little brown donkey with beads and bells –" And then Ariadne giggled and gazed all the way up to his darkly handsome face. "You look nice today, Patir."

"Flattery, young woman, will not buy you a donkey until you are old enough to take proper care of an animal larger than the pup." He glanced at Hebe with a directness that made his eyes seem brilliantly cold and dark. "The walk home is a long one, Miss Lawnay, so will you take a cab? I suggest one with a horse in front of it, as Ariadne is feeling in an equestrian mood." He held out a hand with a selection of coins taken from his pocket. Hebe accepted them, and felt Daphne studying her from under the brim of her hat, down-tilting to flatter her creamy face and painted eyelids. She was staring hard, as if Hebe's slim, fair youth had become a real threat to her plans. Her gaze was sharp, as if in her expensive suit, with shoes and handbag beautifully matched, she felt overdressed by comparison with Hebe's simple, almost flimsy summer dress, a mere shift of inexpensive silk, revealing her slim arms and legs, and her slender neck.

149

Her neck felt bared for the sword under that look of Daphne's!

It was no surprise that Daphne should stroll into Hebe's bedroom the following morning. Her abundant hair was glossy against the rich silk of her robe, and her eyes looked younger without the applied lashes and the mauve colouring.

"Mmm," she took a slow look around the room, "I wondered what your boudoir was like. In fact, it's rather like the chaste white cell of a novice."

Hebe turned from the dressing-table, already dressed and alert for battle. She had just combed her hair and a bright wing of it fell over her left eye.

"Good morning," she said, in a bright voice. "The weather looks good again – are you going swimming this morning?"

Daphne's gaze travelled all the way over the younger girl, taking in her tawny hair, the barest hint of curves beneath the muslin-look blouse embroidered with leaves. Her waist was narrow as a boy's, encircled by a buckled belt. The flare of her short skirt was young and free.

"My dear Hebe," Daphne gave her throaty laugh, "I am not the outdoor type, as you must already be aware. I don't enjoy being tousled and sea-blown, with sand in my hair. On you it doesn't matter. In some ways you're still a child, and that is why Ariadne likes you."

Daphne paused in front of the enamelled icon on the wall, its softly burning colours depicting the Virgin of the Repose.

"Because you make a playful companion for the daughter, you mustn't run away with the idea that you'd make an exciting mate for the father. You are young in your ways, and will remain so for quite a time to come;

Nikos is like me. We both have some wreckage in our lives to make up for. We're both adult to a degree beyond your unworldly vision. We click, he and I." Daphne turned slowly to look at Hebe and her smile was a warning and a victory. "We look good together and amuse each other."

As she allowed these words to sink in, she raised a hand on which the green gem sparkled and touched the lobe of her left ear, which was crimson ... as if lips had been kissing it.

"Nikos always fascinated me, even when Cicely had him ... strange how from a distance you could be mistaken for her. That may be why he notices you now and then, because the outer Hebe has that peachiness she had. That fair-skinned delicacy – but he learned, poor Nikos, that he should never have married her. She had prettiness but no passion. She liked to be admired, but she didn't like to be touched – in case she bruised. No man can tolerate that kind of wife for ever, especially a Greek with lightning in his veins and thunder in his soul."

Hebe took up the hair buckle that matched the one on her belt and she clipped her hair into it, her eyes lowered so she didn't have to meet Daphne's gaze. "Do you believe ...?" She bit her lip, for to say the words was to give them life, and night and day she wondered ... *was it true?* Had he in anger, or impatience, caused Cicely to fall to her death?

"What do you think?" Daphne spoke softly, insinuatingly. "You can see the kind of man he is. He's capable of loving a woman until nothing exists for her except his love – he gave that love to a pretty little doll, not particularly wise or witty, though she was likeable enough. The sort who should live in a silk-lined box and not have to face the real facts of marriage with a real man. In company

151

they were gay and sparkling and the focus of all eyes – but no play goes on for ever, no supper at the club lasts until dawn. When they went home to their smart and ultra-modern apartment, they were alone. I dread to think, dear Hebe, what their life was like – when they were alone."

"So you believe . . .?"

Daphne shrugged her curvaceous shoulders beneath the flowered silk that swept to her ankles in graceful frills. "There are many things on this earth that heaven has to bear with grace, but quite frankly I don't think of Nikos as a devil, I think of him as a tortured angel. Hebe, do I make you catch your breath? Didn't I say once before that he reminds me of the Angel Gabriel? That dark and haunting face, those eyes that could hide heaven or hell. I ask no questions, of him or myself. I believe –"

She paused and her smile held mystery and a luxurious hint of love. "Yes, I do believe I could give up the world and all its false joys for the sake of Nikos Stephanos. He and his arms would be world enough for me – a taste of wine and honey after the sweet smell of Chanel and champagne. Devil or saint, Nikos is very much a man, and it was so amusing yesterday to hear his child asking you to be his wife."

Daphne laughed, but Hebe recalled that yesterday she had received Ariadne's remark in frozen silence, and she had looked at Hebe as if her charm could hide a certain cruelty.

"I guess she still remembers Cicely, in her infant way, and confuses your image with her mother's. It's natural enough for the child, but Nikos is unlikely to be so con-fused." Daphne glanced at the bedside clock. "My, is that the time already? Zea will have brought up my breakfast and I hate congealed eggs! I must say I've enjoyed our little chat, Hebe. How about you?"

"I wouldn't have missed it," Hebe said dryly. "Daphne, may I say something?"

"Feel at liberty, my dear." Daphne stood with languid grace by the door, holding it ajar. Her smile was indulgent, but the pupils of her eyes were sharp, like diamonds that could cut. The emerald on her hand flashed green fire against the pale grip of her knuckles.

"I may be unworldly," said Hebe, "but I wonder why women always assume that because they admire a man, every other woman sees him as some sort of a god. I don't need to be warned against Nikos Stephanos . . . he couldn't be more of a contrast to the sort of man I like. I find petrifying the entire look of him!" Hebe clenched her hands, as if to crush that sensation left in them of a shoulder like iron, and skin that struck warm, black-fleeced through the opening of a white shirt.

"I – I wasn't amused by Ariadne's request. It was like some awful moment in a nightmare, when someone blurts out a secret you hoped would never be revealed . . . and in front of all those people! I wanted the sands to open and swallow me . . ."

"Which I imagine would have been far more uncomfortable – ah, I beg your pardon, Daphne!"

"Nikos!"

Both Hebe and Daphne looked startled as Ariadne erupted into the room followed by the tall figure of her father, who must have been right outside the door when Hebe had spoken. His eyes mocked her startled look while Daphne was given a courteous Greek bow.

"Nounou, guess what! Oh, it is smashing! Patir is taking all of us for a sail on the *caique*, and we'll see the dolphins." Ariadne danced round Hebe and then took a flying leap on the bed. Her hair had not yet been bunched and it swung about like a young witch's.

"Is everyone pleased?" Nikos swept a look from Daphne to Hebe. "The sea is like uncorked wine this morning and the *caique* will sail as smoothly as oil. Well, Miss Lawnay?" His look challenged her. "You have been on the *Kara* once before and found her attractive."

Hebe glanced at Ariadne, whose eyes were sparkling. "If it's perfect sailing weather, then it would be a shame not to take advantage of it. I'd like to see the dolphins as well."

"Excellent. And what do you say, Daphne?" He seemed to lay stress on her name, as if to emphasize the fact that he was not formal with her. "I know you don't like flying, but sailing has a magic no woman can resist."

"I'm all for it, Nikos." The smile she gave him excluded Hebe and the child. "I have the perfect outfit to wear, and I'll lay on the deck of your boat and get beautifully tanned."

"The *Kara* will be honoured to have on board three attractive young women instead of her usual assortment of cargo." A smile quirked his lip. "Perhaps, Miss Lawnay, when my daughter has stopped bouncing like a yo-yo on your bed, you will do something about that wild mop of hair. Then you must have breakfast while Alik and I put provisions in the jeep."

"The jeep?" Daphne echoed.

"Why yes," he said. "My car has some engine trouble and I haven't the time to see to it."

"I hope we shan't be bumped all over the place on that steep road," she said.

"Come," the white line of his teeth showed for a moment, "where is your sense of adventure?" He drew

154

Daphne from the room and the sound of their voices mingled as they walked away. Hebe fingered the buckle of her belt . . . had he looked annoyed for a moment, or had she imagined it?

"Nounou," Ariadne bounced off the bed, "won't we have fun?"

"Yes, sweetheart, and do come and sit on the stool while I make you look less like an animated golliwog."

"I want a ponytail today, Nounou, and some of your scent. It's all cool when you spray it."

Hebe grinned and took up the hair brush. "Are you going to wear this pea-green sunsuit, or the cherry and white?"

"No, the green, because it matches your eyes." Ariadne hummed to herself while her hair was brushed and tailed. "Oh, Nounou, I can't wait to see the dolphins. Patir knows where they go to play and he's taking us there. Isn't he kind today?"

"I'm sure he's always kind to you, Dee. He loves you very much and that's why he wanted you to come and live with him. He wasn't being unkind when he took you away from America."

"It's better now you're here." Ariadne leaned back on the stool and rested her head against Hebe, then she said in a hush-hush voice: "I don't like Daphne very much. She pats me just like I pat Curly, and all the time she talks to me she's looking at Patir. She said I looked like him."

"Well, he's your father, Dee."

"My mother was pretty, Nanna said so. I remember that she had golden hair, but she would never let me touch it. Why do people die, Nounou? I thought people had to be old before they died, but my mother was young like you."

Hebe had hoped and prayed that Ariadne would never

155

ask this question, and now she must be very careful how she replied. Her reply would be tested later against the rumours that would never die easily. "When we are born, Dee, we don't know how big the world is, and how filled it is with things that can make us happy or sad. It's like Curly. If you didn't take care of him, he might fall off the cliffs. When we grow up we have to take care of ourselves, and sometimes we don't do this very well and we fall and hurt ourselves, and sometimes we die. The world is our big garden and we are as fragile as butterflies and bees. Just as a butterfly can break a wing, or a bee drown himself in a rain puddle, so can we. Only our garden is so much bigger, and the sea is so much deeper – do you understand, Dee?"

Ariadne gnawed her lip in thought, intelligent enough to have been told the plain facts of life and death, and yet with a sensitive imagination which Hebe wished to safeguard. There was world enough and time for Ariadne to face the brutal facts, and it did no harm to let her imagine the world as yet as an enchanted wood where castles reared their silver towers.

She looked at Hebe and nodded. "It's like ladybirds . . . if you don't blow them off your arm they get crushed. And worms are so silly the way they crawl off the flower beds on to the paths . . . like people walking into the road where the cars are. But I don't like wasps. They're like angry people who scold all the time." Suddenly it had become a game and a wide smile spread across Ariadne's face. "Patir is like a dragonfly, zooming around and bossing all the flowers, and sort of bronzy. Don't you think?"

"I think, young lady, that if we don't soon go down to our breakfast, he and Daphne will go off on the *caique* without us."

"No fear!" Ariadne dashed to the door and went flying off along the gallery to the stairs. Hebe dropped a swimsuit into her raffia bag and followed her to the kitchen. There they quickly ate yogourt and fruit, while the puppy barked with excitement.

"Are you taking him?" Nikos demanded, downing hot coffee and a crusty knuckle of bread thick with honey.

"He'll cry all day if I leave him behind," said Ariadne.

"Then mind he doesn't fall overboard. Zea, you packed a cheese pie in that basket, and the wine?"

"*Ne, kyrios.* The vineyard wine and not the ouzo, as you directed. And lemonade for the child. You are sure of the *meltemi*? The radio did warn –"

"We shall be on our way home before the *meltemi* decides to get rough. You have no jacket, Miss Lawnay?" His eyes flicked her bare arms. "The sun will be hot over the water and you don't want sunburn."

"I have some protective lotion in my bag," she said. "It's most effective."

"Ah, I might have guessed that you would not permit yourself to go unguarded on my *caique*." His eyes met hers and glinted a dual meaning. "If you have had enough to eat, the jeep awaits, and I am sure you won't mind sitting at the back with the young people?"

"Not at all, *kyrios*." She wiped the honey from Ariadne's lips, and she felt him there in the doorway, gazing intently at her fair head bent close to the child. She didn't dare to look up until he withdrew into the arcade that led round to the courtyard, where the jeep would be parked.

"Now do you want to run upstairs before we leave?"

Ariadne danced from one foot to the other. "No ... yes."

"Then do hurry, Dee. Your father is all set to go."

"Hold Curly." Ariadne placed the puppy in Hebe's arms and dashed away. Hebe gave a smile as she caught Zea's glance. "She's excited about the dolphins, so I hope we see them. You will feel lonely all by yourself, Zea."

"Not at all, *kyria*. I have the day and I am going to the village to visit my friend Maria. I am helping her to sew fresh linen for her house, which was damaged. She is a widow like myself, and the *kyrios* was good enough to supply the materials for the rebuilding of her small dwelling. In fact, between the two of us, I believe he has supplied each family with the bricks and cement and the timber for new furniture."

"That's very kind of him!"

"You must not think, *kyria*, that he is trying to buy friendship. He is not a man to care about winning favour . . . you know, as I know, that these same people whom he helps would call away their child if it played with his child."

"Then why . . . ?"

Zea shrugged. "Be wise like a Greek woman and never ask why a man is kind one day and cruel the next. Men are like the *meltemi* . . . either cool or hot."

They went out to the courtyard where Nikos was smoking a cheroot and lazily telling Alik that to expect women to be punctual was to expect a minor miracle. "They inhabit a world in which all clocks tell lies and time has no meaning. It's what keeps them young, Alik, while men grow old waiting for them."

"Mees Lawnay is ready." Alik was staring rather bashfully at Hebe, who looked very youthful in her slip of a blouse and belted skirt, standing there in slim contrast to a rugged stone column of the portico.

"My dears!" Warm and seducing as the sun itself, Daphne swept out from the house, eclipsing Hebe in a dress of palest saxe-blue, the neck and the Camelot sleeves trimmed with tiny garnet buttons. Perhaps it wasn't quite suitable for sailing on a Greek boat, but all the same it was a highly romantic dress, and the face above it was beautifully made-up, and the glistening hair was arranged in a rich scroll that bared the clusters of garnets in the lobes of Daphne's ears.

With debonair assurance that she was looking perfectly stunning she went to Nikos with her left hand outstretched, and handed to Alik the circular straw bag that contained her sunbathing things and all the lotions and aids she would need for the day.

"If I have kept you waiting, Nikos, then you must forgive me. I just couldn't make up my mind which dress to wear."

His eyes flashed over her, missing not a detail of her dress, her sheer nylons, or her coiffure. He was clad himself in a casual indigo shirt and slacks.

"You look superb, Daphne, but I hope you realize that my *caique* is not exactly the Onassis yacht."

She laughed. "I refuse to believe that a Stephanos goes to sea in a barge! Well, shall we be off?"

He handed her into the front seat, while Zea said almost in Hebe's ear: "It is a long time since the *kyrios* so enjoyed himself. I hope, however, that the *meltemi* stays calm while he has the goddess on board the *caique*. She will not look so picturesque with windblown hair and her mascara streaming in the spray."

"Zea, I do believe you'd like that to happen!"

"Well, if he has eyes for her, then he might as well see the cake as well as the sugar-icing."

Hebe was laughing as Ariadne came skipping out of the house. "Come along, child," Nikos called out, and they ran, waving to Zea, to be bundled into the back of the jeep with Alik. Fleecy rugs had been spread for them to sit on, and Ariadne was highly delighted by the adventure of it all.

"You should be fairly comfortable," Nikos said, with a flick of his eyes that made Hebe aware of the brevity of her skirt as she sat down on a folded rug. "The drive takes only about ten minutes to the harbour – please to settle down, Dee, or you will bounce around like a pea in a dish."

For answer Ariadne leaned to him and pressed a fingertip into his cleft chin. "All right, big Daddy."

He looked down at her, ponytailed and clad in peagreen, and the grave laughter flickered in his eyes. "These days you like me a little better, eh, my small daughter? Be sure to put the little dog on a lead when we reach the water." He withdrew and closed the door, and a couple of minutes later he had taken the wheel and the engine throbbed into action. They moved at a smooth pace until they started the downhill run, when the occupants at the back were thrown into a laughing heap, with the puppy scrambling all over them and licking every inch of bare skin in a fury of affection. Comfortable was hardly the word for that spin to the harbour!

Daphne emerged from the front seat with not a hair out of place. "My, you do look ruffled," she smiled at Hebe.

Hebe tossed the hair out of her eyes and saw the *caique* riding at anchor about a mile from the shore. Nikos and Alik carried the food and the rugs to a small launch bobbing by the quayside, and as the wind blew off the sea and tingled in her nostrils, Hebe felt a quickening of her blood, and also a little stab of sadness. Dion would have loved all this, but instead she walked beside Daphne who fussed with a silk headscarf, and clung with a show of helplessness to the hard brown hands of Nikos as he assisted her into the launch.

Hebe jumped in unaided with the puppy, while Alik handed Ariadne into the arms of her father. The wind tangled Hebe's hair and fired its tawny gold as it blew from her brow. What a bore to be beautiful and not to take delight in the sea breezes rippling across your skin! Hebe felt rather sorry for Daphne Hilton, to whom beauty was the reflection of her face and her figure in a mirror . . . or the eyes of a man.

For Hebe it was many other things, some as small as a seashell, or as far away as the stars. Things you could not grasp or possess . . . the gold of the sun, the sparkle of the ocean, and the grace of a *caique* built of oak and mahogany timber; built strong to withstand the unpredictable seas, with a carved balustrade outlining the tiller, and sails stretched taut above the blue and white sides.

The launch sped towards the bold eye painted on the prow of the *Kara*, a symbol as ancient as Greek seamanship, when Jason had searched for the golden fleece.

"And how, Nikos, do we get aboard your own special *Argo*?" asked Daphne.

He turned briefly from the wheel of the launch and his skin, his hair, the indigo blue of his shirt, seemed extra striking against the gold and blue of sky and sea. "We climb aboard by rope ladder, and if you fall I shall be there to catch you."

"Then I might arrange to fall," she said flirtatiously, but her smile was a trifle thin, as if she would have preferred to sit alone with him on a sunlit terrace, looking soignée and perfect, with a long cool drink within reach of her hand.

She wanted Nikos . . . her every glance at him held the veiled message, but she was discovering, thought Hebe, that here in Greece he wasn't the sophisticated club-goer, the perfect dance partner, the worldly business man. He was pure Greek, and the sea was his second home. If Daphne desired him enough, then she was going to have to surrender totally to a man who would provide no more silk boxes in big cities for a wife to live in.

He had taken Petra to his heart, and his solace had become the *Kara*. He might never want again to marry, unless he wished to have a son, and Daphne in her romantic Camelot dress hardly looked the maternal type.

As they approached alongside the *caique*, Hebe saw a man who hungered not for a woman but for the peace and turbulence of the seas; the sudden tempest that could subjugate every desire but the wish to ride out the storm into the halcyon waters once again. The sea, Hebe realized, had become the mistress of more than one embittered man.

A dark-faced seaman leaned from the side of the *caique* and called down some words, which Nikos answered in Greek. Hebe heard him say: "The *meltemi* is of no consequence. We come aboard!"

CHAPTER X

A SUN awning had been stretched above the deck of the *Kara* and the fleecy rugs and cushions tossed to the deck itself, so that at first glance the *caique* resembled the pleasure boat of a *pasha* setting off for a day's sailing.

And it seemed that Nikos was in the mood to act the *pasha* today, for he had hired a seaman to sail the *caique*. They were sailing south of Petra, following the dolphins who at this time of the year seemed to make a playground of the gloriously warm bays of Andelos.

"Nikos, I have an idea!" Daphne rolled over on a rug, the brunette gold of her limbs an attractive contrast to the white sunsuit she had changed into, down in his cabin. "If we are going so near Andelos, why not visit your cousin's home? I hear the garden is fabulous since his wife took it over as a sort of hobby, and I'm sure you'd love them to see Ariadne."

He turned from the rail, and whatever the expression in his eyes it was concealed by the sunglasses he was wearing. Hebe glanced at him and thought they added to his look of natural dominance and mystery; dark like his hair and the shirt that held a gleam of silk in the sunlight flooding the deck.

"It would be nice to see Paul and his family, but they may not be on the island. Paul travels widely for the firm, and Domini likes to go with him now the children are at boarding school." A smile came and went on the firm lips beneath the shielded eyes. "They are a couple who continue to love each other with all the intensity of the first

163

year. They would make all the cynics blush with shame for daring to say that love is only an illusion. For Paul and Domini love is the Grail and they found it together."

"I've heard it said that she's one of the most beautiful and elegant women in Greece."

"She is altogether a lovely person," he replied. "A rare combination of golden looks and a golden heart. Paul was fortunate to find her ... in fact he pursued her like Apollo and carried her off rather against her will ... in the beginning."

"It all sounds wildly romantic," sighed Daphne. "Couldn't we go on the island, just in the hope of seeing them? They sound so fabulously happy that some of their romantic glow might rub off ... you never know," she added, with a long meaning look and a throaty laugh. "Come on, Nikos! You never used to be so – so adamant in your decisions, as if iron has entered your soul. You had so much charm in those Boston days that I envied Cicely no end, and wondered how she managed to cope with you."

Hebe, who was playing snakes and ladders with Ariadne on the bare deck, held her breath and didn't dare to look at Nikos ... and then she just had to, to see if Daphne had jabbed through his armour and drawn blood. He was very calmly lighting a cheroot, as if to demonstrate that his hands were as steady as the *caique* on her course, heading for the golden warmth of Andelos waters.

"Charm belongs to youth," he said, "and I have outgrown both "

"Really, Nikos, you speak as if you had given up all the joys of your very virile manhood! I know that Greek widows almost virtually become nuns when they lose their man, but don't tell me Greeks become monkish when they lose a wife? What a waste of all that stamina, and all that love of beauty. Greeks do love a beautiful woman, don't they?"

"Like all men they can be blinded by it. When we reach Andelos we will anchor in one of the bays, but I don't think we will go ashore. The old house of my mother's is closed and shuttered, and I have a strong feeling that Paul and Domini will be away, perhaps on a visit to his sister who lives in the Caribbean."

His face as he mentioned his mother's house was sombre, and Hebe felt a wild inclination to break in on the conversation and change the trend of it. Was Daphne so insensitive that she couldn't tell from the hard gravity of his features that she was treading on very private property. Couldn't she sense that behind those smoked lenses his eyes were ablaze with anger ... pain ... riven emotions. Andelos stood for all the happiness he had known with his mother, and with Kara, the tomboy cousin who had changed overnight into someone so attractive that a wild Irish plantocrat had pursued her and married her.

What was Daphne trying to do ... provoke Nikos into some kind of revelation of iron-controlled feelings?

"Miss Lawnay?"

Hebe gave a start as he addressed her, in that mockingly formal way, and she glanced at him with eyes that reflected the aqua-green of the sea. Her lips were a little apart, as if she had been on the verge of speech when he had spoken, and in a rather deliberate way he took off his dark glasses and his gaze dwelt upon her mouth, as if he were recalling that moment in the half-dark when she had been the only passenger on the *caique* and had slept a while to awaken with Dion's name on her lips. It seemed as if the memory hung between them as he stood by the rail, all the deep, eternal, cruel mystery of the sea behind his wide shoulders, and above his dark head a few clouds fine as blue smoke drifting across the gold of the sky.

"You do look odd, Hebe." A note of sharpness struck through Daphne's voice. "Are you feeling seasick?"

"No . . . of course not. The sea doesn't affect me in that way."

"Well, I must say you look affected," Daphne drawled. "As if the sea had got into your eyes and was drowning your wits."

At that word – drowning – Hebe gave a visible shudder. "The sea gives rise to strange thoughts, perhaps. What were you about to say to me?" She looked at Nikos and wondered why her heart should beat so strangely fast. She had seen before, and admitted the dark power of his attraction . . . she was immune from it because of Dion . . . but Dion her dear love was colder now than the sea itself, far out of touch and only to be reached by the avenue of memory.

"We're playing, Nounou." Ariadne caught at her hand. "It's your turn to throw the dice."

"Yes, by all means throw the dice," said Nikos, his lip quirking. "It's a suspenseful moment when one shakes the dice box, not knowing if good or dire fortune will emerge. Come, let us see what fate has in store for you."

"All right." She laughed and shook the little box and the dice gave her seven points. She counted along the board and mounted a ladder, only to find a serpent in her path. "There, *kyrios*, you brought me misfortune!"

"It seems a habit of mine, does it not?" He seemed as if he would smile, but instead he took a pull at his cheroot and the strong tobacco tangled with the smell of the ocean and the sun-baked timbers of the *Kara*. Far aloft in the sails the wind made a siren's music, as if it played upon sea harps.

Idyllic morning, thought Hebe, and yet there had been mention of the wind changing suddenly to a music more furious.

"How a sailing ship can stir the imagination," smiled Hebe. "To think of all the history they have made and all the treasure they have carried, from spices to jewels snatched by marauding pirates."

"One can tell from the things that stir your imagination, Hebe, that you are not long out of the schoolroom." Daphne stirred like a lazy tigress on the oriental rug that pampered her while she sunbathed. "Now mine is aroused by living things, by faces and voices, and the exciting differences between men and women."

"You also love jewels," said Nikos, dryly. "Even to sunbathe you wear them."

"Why not, darling, when I have oodles of them? Why keep them locked in a box when they come so alive on a warm-skinned woman? Jewels are living things as well, they are born of myriad substances as we are, and torn from their mother bed to be shaped for life and to give pleasure."

"Not all life is pleasure, *kyria*."

"*Touché*, but not all life is grim reality." She smiled directly into his eyes, for he had not replaced his dark glasses. "Life and ecstasy are twin souls, they give pain and pleasure in equal measure. They are cream and coffee, delicious together, but cloying and bitter if kept apart. Don't you agree, Nikos?"

"Of course." He gave her a slight ironical bow. "How could I disagree with a beautiful woman? It would not be gallant."

"Do you disagree?" she demanded, and she half sat up so that her golden shoulders made a curve above the deep cleavage of her suntop. The garnets burned in her earlobes, and her mouth was a delectable pout of scarlet. She had at a glance a luscious indolence, but a second more intent look would have revealed the stab of her scarlet nails into the soft rug; the dilated pupils of a woman torn by desire.

Hebe was attuned to see these signs because Daphne had told her frankly that she wanted Nikos Stephanos, and the younger girl saw them with an inward shrinking. It wasn't the facts of love that she shrank from, but she sensed that Daphne could be a tigress beneath that smooth golden skin and Hebe could almost feel those long nails ripping *her* skin.

Yet why? She played no part in this drama that for Daphne and Nikos had begun far away in Boston. She was the child's companion . . . the man's reluctant guest. She could not endanger the hopes and plans of Daphne Hilton, for Nikos would take or reject as the will took him!

"How long will it be before we see the dolphins?" Ariadne wanted to know, and Hebe blessed her for the sweet innocent words, like cool water thrown on smouldering flames.

"We should be in sight of them in another couple of hours. Come, *mou,* and sit on the rail beside me and look at the sea." Nikos held open his arms to her. "I want you never to be afraid of it, no matter what mood it might be in."

Ariadne ran to him and he swung her to the rail and held her there in the crook of his brown arm. She ran a hand along his arm and gazed up at his face. "Why are ladies smoother than men?" she asked. Hebe heard a deep ring of affection in his laughter, and it seemed as if Greek men took a great delight in the natural charm of their daughters even though they might regard the life-link of a son as important. Was that why Greek women grew up without inhibition, because in childhood they were held to the beating heart of the father as well as the mother?

"Honey," drawled Daphne, "most little girls are made of satin and spice and all things nice. Boys are put together with corks and screws and monkey tails."

Ariadne burst into giggles and pressed her face against the side of her father's neck. He quirked an eyebrow at Daphne above his daughter's head. "You should have had a child, *kyria*. Something of your own to cherish and amuse, and be amused by."

"Oh, there's plenty of time for all that, Nikos. You don't imagine that I intend to remain devoutly widowed like a Greek woman, do you? My dear man, it's all too pagan for words, as if a woman married a soulmate instead of a living, breathing, very earthy male. And besides, black is not my colour. It isn't many a woman's colour, for that matter, unless the black is a gorgeous velvet and she is divinely fair like –" Daphne stopped speaking, but her broken words remained in the air. She had been about to mention Cicely, whose pale golden hair and fair skin would never have turned sallow when contrasted with a rich black velvet, dense as the eyes of the man she had loved. . . .

"I – I do hope the weather continues to be fine," said Hebe. "I'm looking forward to a swim later on."

"I was going to ask if you had brought a bathing suit with you," said Nikos, and his eyes seemed to flash a message of gratitude that she had turned the talk away from personal matters. "The waters of Andelos are like silk and you must not depart from Greece without having swum in 'Apollo's pool' where frolics his 'desire of the sea.'"

"The dolphins," she said. "All grace and gentle-hearted."

"Exactly. And now I suggest that we open the provision basket, Alik, and see what your mother has given us."

"I could go for a cool lager and lime," said Daphne. "But I suppose, you iron-hearted Greek, I must take whatever you are prepared to give me?"

"There is lemonade, I believe." His smile held a hint of the sardonic. "You must remember, Daphne, that we Greeks are basically Spartan in our tastes."

"A loaf of bread, olives and wine in the wilderness, Nikos?"

"Yes, why not? Alik, please to pour wine for the *kyria* and myself." He glanced at Hebe. "You will prefer lemonade, of course. It is crushed from our own lemons and sweetened with wild honey, and I requested that Zea pack a flask of ice cubes."

"Sounds delicious . . ." And it was, in a long glass that melted the ice slowly while she stood by the rail and let her eyes drink in the many shades of blue and green that merged in the water. The untamed enemy of man yet which offered a transient peace when the waves ran like uncoiled silk, and the tips of the waves glittered as if jewelled. Nikos had spoken of her departure as if it might be imminent, and indeed the days were passing quickly, and this day held an intangible quality of delight and un-rest that she would remember when other quieter days had slipped from her memory. Words and glances had taken on a significance only fully realized now a quietness

170

had fallen upon the party while they quenched a thirst made sharp by the salt in the sea air.

Hebe took deep lungfuls of the air and felt that dizzy intoxication of one glass of wine too many, yet she only drank icy lemonade. Like Ariadne and Alik she must not be given the potent Greek wine from a wild vineyard on a sun-soaked hillside, or perhaps from the garden of one of those stony monasteries. She was young and English and untried, yet she knew enough to know that today on board the *Kara* the forces of drama were at work; a whisper of excitement, even of danger, lay curled within the beauty of the day like a worm within the bud, and it was not entirely due to the words the Greek sailor had called to Nikos as they came aboard. The *meltemi* blew daily and there was always the chance that it would blow into a tempest . . . what Hebe felt was almost sensory, like the brush of a fine cobweb against her skin, pulling her to the centre of a web fate had started to spin before she ever came to Greece.

Hebe stared at the glistening sea, and once again her heartbeats were almost audible to herself, like tiny drumbeats of warning there in her slight young bosom.

She pressed to the rail, as if solid and sun-warmed it offered the comfort of the tangible; a pressure that might stifle that inward fluttering; that strange new awareness of herself as someone a stranger might hate . . . or love.

Strange how you could live for twenty years and be unaware of yourself as a danger to someone . . . or a delight. She stood there, undefended against the ruthless caress of the sun, gazing at the ardent, tormenting and glorious sea. It was as if she had been sleeping and had suddenly awakened to a new awareness of things. Everything had a more living texture . . . her own reality was more vivid, more alive to the aching pleasure of the sun's caress, against her skin and her eyes. It was as if today she burst fully from the chrysalis which Dion's death had half torn away from her young body and heart . . . as if right now she must test her wings and find them fragile or strong.

The sparkle of the sea held her spellbound, and then her hair whipped across her eyes in a sudden gust of wind, and overhead, where the kingpost held aloft the spread sails, she heard the ropes tauten and felt the *Kara* ride the supple coil of a wave that spattered the deck with spray.

The wind was freshening, and Hebe turned involuntarily to glance at Nikos. He had glanced up at the wheelhouse and exchanged a look with the Greek sailor, and she wondered if they were heading into high winds and whether he would give the order for the *caique* to be turned about. In that brief moment while she watched him, she saw his profile etched in all its pure menace against the blue and gold of the sky, and she knew that he made a rapid and deliberate decision.

He inclined his dark head, and the shoulders of the seaman lifted in a brief but eloquent shrug. So be it! The captain had given his order and the *Kara* continued on her way to Andelos.

Nikos then turned his head before Hebe could look away from him, and she was deeply startled, even shocked, by the brilliance of his eyes. They dwelt on her face, then like a flame they swept her from head to toe.

"Lunch time!" he said crisply, and he took a look at the watch on his wrist, the leather strap only a shade darker than his darkly tanned skin. "By the time we have eaten, we will be almost in sight of Andelos."

She wanted to ask about the wind, which took her hair

as if in a fist and made a golden whip of it. The deep Greek eyes of Nikos narrowed, so that their brilliance seemed more intense. He knew her thoughts, her stab of anxiety, but he said not a word to reassure her. He was forcing her to appeal to him, and she would never do so. He knew her pride, and he wanted to bend it. He was, perhaps, as cruel as she had dared to imagine him.

"I'm hungry as anything," said Ariadne, glancing up from her story book. "And so is Curly."

"Yes, let's eat," said Daphne. "All this sea air does whip up the appetite."

It whipped up the emotions as well, thought Hebe, and she tautened as Nikos asked her to help serve the food.

"Yes, of course." She walked towards him, aware of the deck beneath her feet and each separate moment that brought her closer to him. There was a certain arrogance in the way he stood, legs braced to take the motion of his ship. The *Kara* rode the deepening swells with her sails spread proudly against the Greek sky. They seemed, man and ship, to be welded together in strength and defiance, and Hebe saw in each a raking grace which could not be denied.

"I hope you don't mind that I ask for your assistance?" he said.

"Why should I mind?" Irresistibly she glanced at Daphne, whose lazy abandonment to the sun was not to be disturbed by the mundane duty of serving up food. "I'm glad to be of use."

"Youth is restless," he murmured, and for the briefest of wicked moments he smiled into her eyes. "In body and mind, and now live up to your name and be my serving maid."

She was bereft for a second of a suitably stinging
173

answer, then she said what she felt impelled to say each time she looked at him. "*You* are no god . . . the opposite would be true of you!"

"And now having said it do you feel better?" he enquired.

"Yes, I feel fine." But in truth she felt defiant, and always that bit unsure of what he really was. He lifted the big food basket on to a hatch-cover and put back the lid that held inside it the plates and cutlery. He handed her the various containers of food and she took them to the sun-awning. She returned for the plates and the check tablecloth, and felt Daphne's eyes boring through the thin material of her blouse, raking her legs beneath the short hem of her skirt, seeing her as a female rival for the attentions of Nikos Stephanos.

"I will bring the pickles and fruit," he said.

"The sailor will want some lunch." She glanced up at the wheelhouse, at the seaman whose bronzed torso gleamed above his cotton trousers.

"Do you fancy taking it to him?" queried Nikos, and she heard a taunting note in his voice, as if he thought she admired the sun-dark virility of his fellow Greek. "I am sure he would be most flattered to have wait upon him the Anglika with her skein of golden hair, her limpid green eyes, and her body as supple as new silk."

For several seconds Hebe was too shocked for speech, and the green of her eyes darkened as her face went white. "How dare you say such a thing?"

"Why, aren't you flattered? Or are you pretending to be unaware that your looks are the fair mirage, the cool fountain that turns to dry stone at a touch . . ."

"Don't!" She backed away from him, she actively fled to the sun-awning, to a place on the rug beside the child

and the romping animal. She felt as if she had been struck
. . . accused. Tears stung her eyelids and she forced them
into retreat as she put food on a plate for Ariadne; ham
and tomatoes and big boiled shrimps. A little mayonnaise
from the pot, and a crunchy slice of bread and butter.
Curly's meat and gravy were in a small container of their
own, and she busied herself with the child and the dog,
and it was Nikos who took food to the sailor.

"What did he say to you?" The words sprang at her
and she flinched as she looked at Daphne, who held a
speared shrimp on her fork. "Come on, you jumped away
from him like a scalded cat."

"I can assure you he wasn't paying me a compliment,"
Hebe said, and she ducked her head to her plate and forced
herself to eat a piece of ham.

"No," said Daphne, and her voice was like silk. "I don't
know how he can endure to have you around when you
look – I guess it's the salt in the air, but I must have another glass of wine." Daphne switched adroitly to another subject as Nikos came to sprawl beside her and to
help himself to food.

The sun blazed overhead, and yet Hebe felt curiously
cold. She ate her lunch without tasting it, and felt as if
her fair, windblown hair had become the whip across
Nikos' shoulders. There had been no need for Daphne to
complete her indictment . . . how could he bear to endure
someone who reminded him constantly of the wife he had
loved . . . the girl who had turned his love to a cruel thrust
of the hand?

Why did he endure her? Hebe had not asked to stay
within his sight, in his home, on his ship, close enough for
his child to lay a fond head against her bare arm, tickling
her with fawn-soft hair.

"I'm terribly happy," Ariadne whispered. "Are you, Nounou?"

Hebe hesitated only a fraction of a moment before she nodded her head ... the child's day was going to stay unclouded even if hers had been spoiled. "Yes, I feel tops, Dee!" She said it gaily and hoped she was overheard by Daphne, who was basking in the sole attention of Nikos. Alik had gone up to the wheelhouse to keep the sailor company, and a transient peace brooded over the *caique*.

"And now what do you fancy for dessert?" Hebe asked the child. "An orange, a fig, or some of those big black cherries?"

"Cherries!"

And knowing half of them would soon adorn the small ears, Hebe also peeled an orange and they ate it between them.

"You will not have a slice of this cheese pie?" Nikos enquired, meeting her eyes with his dark eyes, in which still lurked those tiny gleams of mockery.

"No, thank you. I have had all I can take." And she said it with a stress on the words and she was not referring to food. In her raffia bag she carried the wallet which held her money and her passport. They were heading for Andelos and she would stay there overnight, buy some clothes in the morning and catch the steamer to the mainland and the airport. She left nothing of value at the Villa Helios, only a few summer outfits and some lingerie. Her only regret was that she must leave Ariadne. She was a delightful child and couldn't help it that she had an arrogant devil for a father!

"Look at me, Patir." Ariadne danced about the sunlit deck with double-stemmed cherries swinging from her ears. The puppy romped excitedly about her ankles, and

176

Hebe was smiling when it happened . . . when the little dog ran too near the railings of the deck and fell through the lower opening into the sea.

Ariadne screamed and her small face went as white as paper. Hebe leapt to her feet a moment before Nikos, and obeying swiftly the instinct to help small things in distress she ran to the ship's rail, kicking off her sandals, unzipping her skirt and diving in after the puppy in what seemed a single motion, a split second of time, even as a voice thundered her name.

The water struck her in the face and she was swept into the motion of a glistening wave and she gasped aloud, then her eyes were clear again and she struck out towards the tiny dark object that struggled in all that rolling expanse of water.

CHAPTER XI

It was the hands of Nikos that dragged her on board the launch. In her arms whimpered the wet, frightened puppy.

"You foolish girl!" She was gripped and shaken like a wet rag doll. "You impetuous animal-lover! You could easily have struck your head against the side of the *caique* and been drowned!"

"B-but I didn't." She said it bravely and breathlessly as he allowed her to sit down. She cradled Curly against her wet and clinging slip as a blanket was slung around her and fingers brushed flamy across her bare shoulders and dragged her drenched hair outside the folds of the blanket. "M-mind Curly, or you'll smother the poor mite."

"I could smother you!" The words came savagely, half-strangled above her head, and she glanced up, blinking water from her lashes, and looked into eyes so blazingly angry that she shrank away from them. "Is it what you want . . . to be drowned? Are you like her in every way –?" The words broke off and yet they went on throbbing in the air between them, while the launch bobbed on the water and the sun was suddenly clouded over.

The cloud darkened his face and made it seem relentless, and then abruptly he touched her cheek, and the drooping ears of the puppy. Then he swung away from her and with a thrust of his hand on the controls he sent the launch speeding towards the *caique*.

Down in his cabin Hebe dried herself with a large towel,

178

and she put on a shirt of his, and a pair of denim jeans belonging to Alik, which hugged her hips and legs while the shirt hung over her shoulders and the sleeves over her wrists. She rolled up the sleeves, and then she brushed her hair and clipped its dampness away from her neck. She stared at her face in his shaving mirror and saw how strange her eyes looked, bright and yet dazed, like those of a person who had suffered a shock and been given a heady drink to offset the effects of the shock.

She had been given brandy from a flask, which he had forced her to drink. It had made her gasp and burn . . . or had she burned because his hands had touched her again, grasping her chin and demanding that she obey him this time and do as she was told. With Daphne looking on she had felt more like the bedraggled puppy than a heroine!

Hebe went on deck, where she found the puppy being carefully dried by Nikos, while Ariadne hung over her rescued pet and crooned words of love. "You're all right now, darling Curly. You're safe with Dee and my big Daddy."

And then she spotted Hebe and ran to her with eager, outstretched arms. She hugged Hebe as if she would become part of her. "Darling Nounou! Oh, you are the bravest, most smashing person in all the world a-and I do love you!"

"I love you, Dee." And as Hebe held the child she felt grateful that for a while she had been able to give her care and affection, but she could not change the plans she had made before Curly's mishap. It was imperative that she leave the Greek islands and return home to England, to a career that would soon help her to forget this strange idyll . . . the man who in every way was "a pagan son of dark sorrows."

She must go home to familiar things, to faces less powerfully striking, and try to forget how her heart had leapt, as if trying to reach him, when he had asked savagely if she was like Cicely in every way.

Yes, he had meant his wife ... the young and lovely foreign woman who had died among the harsh stones of Petra.

It was then that she saw the first dolphin, curving its long body in a glistening blue-grey acrobatic, thrusting its inquisitive snout high in the air as the *caique* sailed by.

"Look, Dee! Isn't he a beauty?"

"Dolphins!" Ariadne dashed to the ship's side and hung her head through the rails. "Nounou, isn't he big and shiny ... he's turning a somersault!"

"Child, don't hang through those rails," Nikos commanded. "We don't want Miss Lawnay diving in for a second rescue, not with those great creatures about. There's another, which means we are sailing close to Andelos."

He came and handed the puppy to Hebe, then he sat the child on the rail and held her firmly, while Daphne strolled over to stand close to him. "They are rather amusing, aren't they?" she drawled. "I reckon you could keep a small dolphin in that sunken Roman pool of yours, Nikos. It would keep the youngster amused."

He was silent a moment as he gazed at the dolphins, the ocean's most lovable and sportive creatures. "No creature is happy, Daphne, kept apart from those to whom it belongs, and deprived of the environment into which it was born. It pines for the life it has known."

Hebe kept her gaze on the playful dolphins, a fairly large school of them, as the lyre-shaped island of Andelos

180

hove into view. Now she seemed to hear in every word spoken by Nikos a reference to his wife. She caught the brooding note of regret, the thread of pain, and she knew that he was haunted by his insistence that Cicely leave America and live as the wife of a true Greek.

Being so truly Greek he had pined for what he loved . . . Greece the beautiful and the cruel, sun-silvered amid the fiery rock, where the quail were led to safe nesting by the night ravens. Where the markets were not super but old and colourful. Where the fragrances were earthy, clinging to the senses and disturbing them. Where life was more primitive and emotional, the palate for living not blunted by packaged food and the false glitter of modern existence.

Had it come slowly, or swiftly, Hebe's realization that the deep strong passions of Nikos Stephanos had met in Cicely a stream of feeling so shallow that it was no wonder their marriage had foundered on the Rock of Helios and ended there in disaster.

The *caique* was anchored just off the island where Nikos had been born and where he had run wild as a boy. They came ashore in the launch and Hebe crossed the sands to a rock behind which she could change into her swimsuit. It was jade-green, laced at the sides, and so heavenly cool after the leg-hugging jeans and the over-large shirt. As she slipped the straps over her bare shoulders she seemed to feel again the touch of hard male fingers against her skin, and she closed her eyes as there shot through her very bones an exquisite kind of torture never felt before.

It was the atmosphere of the Greek islands, she told herself. The sun and the wind; the warmth and the savage beauty. They aroused the senses and made the body aware of itself. A plunge into the sea would soon dispel such a strange, unwanted longing, and she ran . . . ran as if pursued, into the churning silk of the surf, into the embrace of the lively sea.

The inner bay waters were delicious to swim in, and even Daphne, after strapping on a white cap, joined them and swam with a touch of that lazy luxuriance so much a part of her. Nikos in black briefs was like some bronze savage, a pagan *kouros* moulded from the molten gold of the sun itself. He struck like a lance through the water, cleaving strongly the rise and fall of the outer waves, until his surge of the elemental seemed satisfied and he swam with his child straddling the naked power of his shoulders.

Hebe floated on her back and saw as in a tilted mirror the *caique* in restless movement, chained by her anchor, the sea sparkling and foaming about her painted sides. The sunlight rippled over her sails, and the sound of Alik's *bouzouki* drifted across the water. He had chosen to stay aboard with the sailor and to listen to his tales of travel, and Hebe remembered how Dion had loved to listen to the old sailormen down on the shore, yarning away as they mended the fishing nets, seamed and sea-weathered as the old boats themselves.

In that moment the sun clouded over again, and a shiver ran all through Hebe, from the ends of her wet hair to her gently moving heels. She turned swiftly over in the water and swam to the shore, where she wanted suddenly to hide away from the sight of the *Kara*. It made her too aware of the return journey to Petra; of the rather fearful moment when she must say to Nikos:

"I'm not coming with you . . . nor can you force me to come. I'm going home from Andelos to my own country, to my career." And then she would use the weapon he had himself placed in her hands. "You said yourself,

182

Nikos Stephanos, that no creature is happy away from its own environment."

She lay in the shade of an oleander bush, and as the sound of Ariadne's laughter came to her across the sands she closed her eyes tightly to hold back the tears. How lonely England would seem, without Dion, and without Dee. How unutterable without ever again the sound of a deep voice saying mockingly: "Miss Lawnay!"

She lay prone as a jade idol while the stunning truth swept over her and took away her breath. And as those waves of truth swept over her again and again, she felt the disbelief of the drowning person, the panic to struggle against the engulfment, and then the surrender that left her weak upon the sands.

When had it started . . . or had there never been a beginning, only this final recognition of what could never be?

Why had she never guessed that whenever she fought with him she had been fighting herself, thrusting from her thoughts his face and trying to impose upon it the image of Dion? But Dion, no matter how dear he had been to her, had been but a boy. Nikos was a man, and so he aroused in her a woman's feelings. A man who had known marriage with another woman. A man accused . . . a sinner, they said, who alone knew the secret of his guilt or his innocence.

She lay quiescent after the inner tumult of her confession to herself; this her secret, as sin or slander might be his. This her storm, faced alone beneath the oleanders, pink and lush amid their deep green leaves . . . and then suddenly tossed in a scatter of scented petals by a furious breath of wind.

Hebe sat up and saw a great blue-green curve of water

183

rushing up the beach to where Ariadne played with the sand. Hebe jumped to her feet and ran to the child, and together, the small body pressed to her, they were drenched in that tidal wave. It receded, but in a moment it would return, and they fled away from it up the beach. A big rock jutted there and they sped round it, and were brought up short by the sight of Nikos holding Daphne by the hands while she strained towards him. "I never once stopped thinking about you," she was saying. "All the time, whenever we met, and afterwards when you left. Nikos, I can give you substance, darling, not shadow!"

He stared down at her, and he must have gripped her hands so hard that she winced with pain. He seemed to be holding her, and himself in check, and the passion blazed so warmly in Daphne's eyes that anything might have happened if Ariadne and Hebe had not broken in on their absorption ... the child crying out the Greek word for father.

Even as he turned a startled head, a violet glare of lightning licked across the sea, running like livid flame along the tips of the high waves, and seeming to find a place in his eyes, flickering there as he looked at Hebe.

"It looks as if the *meltemi* has hit us with a vengeance. What do we do, *kyrios*, find shelter under the cliffs or return to the *caique*?" She spoke with a gay bravado above the sudden tumult of the wind, for no one, least of all Nikos, must see the love, crouching as if from a blow at seeing him with Daphne.

He stood there with the wind whipping at his black hair, gazing out to where the rising sea whipped at the *Kara*, rocking her to and fro. Even as they watched her sails were being furled, and the other anchor would be dropped to hold her secure while the *meltemi* tore the day to shreds and the sun drew blue-grey clouds around its brightness.

"What do we do, Nikos?" Daphne clutched at his bare arm. "The launch will bounce like a cork over that rough sea – oh, Nik, I'm scared!"

"We must all get dressed, at once!" he said. "Stay here, I will fetch your things."

He dived through the wind and the stinging whips of water, and returned swiftly with Hebe's shirt and jeans, his own clothes, and Daphne's sunsuit. "Put them on over your swimwear," he ordered.

"My bag," said Hebe, shouting above the wind. "Did you bring that?"

"Ah, I must have missed it."

"I must have it!" She ran, curving her body against the lash of wind and sand, and made for the rock where she had undressed and left her raffia bag, holding her money and her passport, those precious means of escape from Nikos. Waves were thundering up the beach by now, driven impetuously forward by the powerful and angry wind. And Hebe saw that she was racing them towards the rock, that her bag and what it held would be snatched away from her. Even as she spurted into the very path of that great surge of angry water, a pair of arms caught roughly hold of her and she was lifted off her feet by a male force, as purposeful as the sea that would have battered her slim body against that jutting rock.

"My bag!" She pummelled him in the storm, in the flying spray that fell on their skin like rain, in the flair of lightning over his wet face and ruffled hair. She fought with him, there in the mad heart of the *meltemi*, and the straps of her swimsuit were half off her shoulders in the struggle, and her lips were stung and glowing against the pallor of her face.

Then suddenly he bent his head and with savage insistence he held her against his bare wet chest and fiercely he crushed her lips with his.

"You little wildcat! I will make you purr for me for once!" Each word was mingled with each pressure of his lips against her face, her throat, the lobes of her ears. It was unbelievable, yet it was real ... the heavens ripped open by steel fingers of lightning while a man and a girl clung and kissed for wild and endless moments.

Hebe knew dazedly that the waves must be carrying her handbag away, just as Nikos was carrying her, but it no longer seemed to matter. When he lowered her to her feet she swayed and clutched his shoulder, so hard and vital, and warmly wet.

"Nikos?" she whispered.

"This is no time for us to talk," he said.

Daphne must have seen them, clasped so close in the battering of the wind, when nerve had leapt to meet nerve, and their hearts had thrilled into a single beating force.

His hard fingers closed over Daphne's white-clad shoulder. "You will say nothing hurtful, for there has been enough of that. The storm will last about an hour, then we will go home."

"Home?" drawled Daphne. "To that solitary house of yours, Nikos, on the crest of that stony Greek hill? No wonder when you took Cicely there she went off her head —"

"Be quiet!" he ordered. "You will not mention her name again!"

Daphne gave a shrug and a husky laugh. "You must be a born martyr, Nik, to let yourself be taken in again by a golden-haired doll. Look at her! She's like a kitten dragged out of a rain barrel!"

Hebe shivered and drew Ariadne close to her. Her hair was wet and straight about the slimness of her neck, and the masculine shirt hid the slight curves Nikos' hard body had bruised for endless, ecstatic moments.

"I am looking," he said, and there slumbered in his eyes the memory of those moments they had shared. Then he bent and lifted Ariadne into his arms. He held her close to him, she and the puppy, and he stroked her hair. "The storm will soon be over, *mou*, and then all will be still and calm and the wind will have polished the stars until they shine like diamonds."

Ariadne encircled his neck with her free arm and whispered something in his ear. He looked a little sombre as he looked directly into Hebe's eyes. "The little one doesn't want you to go away," he said.

Hebe bit her lip and gazed down the beach, from this shelter behind their escarpment of rock. "I – I may be stranded," she said. "My money and my passport are in my bag."

"And that was why you tried to reach it?"

"Yes."

"So you could leave?"

"Yes."

He said no more while the storm raged around them, and when it finally died away they went down the beach to the launch, and by the strangest of chances they found her bag lodged among the stones where the launch was tied. Its contents were soaking wet and covered in sand grains, but her wallet was fast closed and only the edges of her passport had suffered damage.

She held it tightly clenched in her hand . . . and then she stepped aboard the launch and cast a good-bye look at Andelos.

187

She watched the polished stars with Nikos while Ariadne lay asleep in his cabin. Daphne sat smoking while Alik played *bouzouki* music. Now a caressing night breeze blew across the water, and they were becalmed, silent, committed to a peace that must not be broken by words, not just yet.

The *caique* stole through the night like a pirate ship, and put into harbour when everyone seemed abed and fast asleep. They drove home and found Zea anxiously awaiting them, the coffee pot simmering on the stove and ready at once to slake their thirst. Hebe put Ariadne to bed, and was rocking on her own feet when she went to her own bedroom. She didn't dare to think about tomorrow, and fell asleep thinking about the day that had just passed.

Daphne left the Villa Helios the following morning, and as it happened Hebe was alone with her in the few minutes before she climbed into the cab. She had refused to be driven to the village in the jeep, for Nikos had not yet found time to see to his car.

As she stood there, elegant in a suit of cream linen, with a brown straw hat shading her eyes, she had a worldly air entirely out of keeping with the wild Greek landscape. "I hope," she said to Hebe, "that you manage to keep the tiger now you've climbed on his back. Cicely fell off, all the way down that gorge where that sacrificial stone stands. They say he pushed her . . . but that was after she went crazy."

"Please," begged Hebe, "don't go away saying bitter things."

"I feel a little bit that way, honey." The painted, brim-shaded eyes swept over Hebe's pensive face. "I might have got the guy if you hadn't come along with your kitten-gold hair and your buttering up of the kid."

"Good-bye." Hebe held out her hand, but Daphne ignored it and slid into the cab with a luxurious display of silken leg. The door clapped shut and as the cab drove off, Hebe walked round to the side of the house, to the path that led up the hillside. Ariadne would be all right with Zea, and Hebe knew that she was being drawn by the force of love itself to where Nikos was.

She made her way without haste through the thyme and the scented sage, feeling the pull of the ground as it elevated.

She saw him standing alone by the Rock of Helios, his dark head outlined against the blue Grecian sky. She approached him quietly and when she reached his side he turned his head to look at her, young and golden in her simple white dress.

"You came to ask, didn't you? Your desire for the truth is stronger than your desire for me?"

She shook her head. "I believe I already know what happened. Your regret, Nikos, is that you forced her to come to Greece. You blame yourself for what happened here, and you allow others to blame you, because you insisted that she live with you on this island she found so rugged after the gaiety of Boston."

"She was my wife, the mother of my child. I hoped that our Greek sun would melt her, but instead it –"

Hebe quickly lifted a hand and placed it softly against his lips. "Don't speak of it, Nikos. Don't reopen the wound but let it heal and fade away to a very small scar."

"The trouble is," he sighed, "that I am a Stephanos and we seem to love with almost too much love. We seem to possess with almost too much passion. Cicely and I – we should never have met, let alone have married, then one of us might have found a little happiness."

189

"Don't you feel that you will ever be happy?" Hebe asked wistfully.

He gazed down at her for lingering seconds, and then as if he could no longer endure to hold back, he reached for her and it was as it had been during the storm – only stormier.

"I love you – how I love you! I want you, and don't dare to have you."

Yet with her arms twined about his neck she was pressed to him as if he would have contact with her heart as well as her body. "There is the young man Dion. There is your untouched youth – my wreck of a marriage. There is a world beyond Petra for you to explore. There is Greek passion, and you might be afraid of it."

"Do I seem afraid?" she murmured. "Do I tremble, Nikos?"

His lips ran their fire along the smooth skin at the side of her neck, and his breathing was like the soft thunder in the neck of a flower. "What of Dion, of whom you dreamed on my very boat?"

"He died before I ever came to Petra. He was my cousin and I loved him dearly, as a girl does. I love you, Nikos, as a woman does ... with a bit of temper thrown in at times, a wilful urge to pull your leg and bite your shoulder." With an incoherent murmur she buried her face against the hard warm muscle and bone of him. "I want to stay to be yours, or I want to go away quickly, before I love you too much."

Firmly then he held her away from him and he searched her face, her eyes, her pleading lips. "Life with a Greek is a bursting skin of wine; a thing of passion and sometimes pain; joy and anger; aggression and surrender. Can you take all that? So fair and slender –"

"Nikos, I am Hebe! Cupbearer to the god!"

"Or the devil." He drew her close again, clasping her as he had in the midst of the storm. His lips and his fingertips held a tender fire as they caressed her. "Will you be mine, Hebe? To hold and cherish and make of you my joy?"

She gazed up at him and saw the dark attraction of his face, but she knew that what she had to give him was deeper, warmer and far more generous than Cicely's desire of the eyes. In the simplest of terms she loved him, and he was hers to love.

"Well, my Hebe, will you be crowned Greek fashion as my wife?"

"How imperial it sounds, my Nikos."

"Ah, say that once again!"

"My Nikos!"

"It sounds so good, and yet it seems too good to be true." His breath sighed across her face. "Dare I marry you, hoping you will love Greece as much as I do? Dare I take a chance on making you so unhappy that like Cicely you will lose all reason and destroy yourself? My hand did not push her, but my desire for Greek air and stone and sunshine surely did. Hebe, I would sooner let you go than force you to stay with me."

"Force me?" With loving hands she pulled his head down to her and kissed passionately the deep line that etched itself in his cheek. "You said yesterday, dear *kyrios*, that no creature is happy away from its own environment. This is true, if that creature is torn from a loving circle. But mine was broken when Dion died. My father and my mother are far away in Africa, and if I went there to them I would be far from all that can make me happy. They are deeply involved in their very important work, and now I wish to make a life of my own. I wish with all my heart to make it with you, Nikos. I loved Greece from the moment I stepped on to its soil and breathed its air like wild wine. I love you, terribly, and I love your child. Darling, tell me something?"

"Anything, my Hebe. I have no secrets from you."

"Why do I never see you smoking a pipe these days?"

"I only do so when I am working or sailing. The smell of it in the house was not liked by —"

"Hush." Hebe traced the outline of his lips with her fingers. "I like the smell of a pipe ... you were lighting one when we first met and that was why I approached you, otherwise I wouldn't have had the nerve. You looked so tall and formidable standing there on the jetty, so ready to snap my head off. Why, Nikos?"

He ran a hand over her tawny hair, drawing a silky strand of it against his face. "Because of this, and the beauty of your eyes. I wanted to refuse to take you to Petra, but you would have asked someone else. The hour would have been late before you arrived and not all men are courteous towards young women travelling alone. I knew you would be safe with me."

"Was I just another package of cargo?" she laughed.

"The most precious I ever carried."

How good that sounded ... and how exciting to meet his eyes a moment before he took her lips in a kiss that bound her to him even before they made their marriage vows and the two crowns of lemon flower were raised above their heads, and her love for him stilled for ever the doubts and the whispers.

Ariadne would laugh with the other children, and the Villa Helios would no longer be a lonely house.